THe TeN

Sleeper Series Book One

Auri Blest

JOA Press LLC

ISBN 9781095003190

For Kevin

CHAPTER 1

N icole leaned over the bathroom vanity and studied her reflection, ignoring the notes scrolling down the right side of the mirror.

She tapped the glass surface, turning off the notifications for the evening. She didn't need the constant reminders. The night was half over, and all was silent.

Is that a pimple?

"Nikki? Nikki, you're not listening to me. Do not disconnect this call. I'm serious. It's quiet right now, but you need to stay alert."

She rolled her eyes. "I hear you. We're fine, but it's been a crazy day."

"Why? Did something happen?"

"No, I'm just tired. It's nothing a hot bath won't cure. A bath I would like to take right now if *someone* would let me." *Ugh . . . it is a pimple, and there's its ugly twin sister.*

"Okay, well, I guess I'll get going. See you in a few hours. And, Nikki?"

It's the stress. Making me break out like I'm a friggin' thirteen-year-old.

"Nikki?"

"Huh?"

"If all else fails, you get the heck out of there. Do you hear me? Find a way out."

"Uh-huh."

"Nikki, what did I just say?"

"I will—I mean, get out. That's what you said. I'm shutting down now."

He sighed heavily. "Okay, see you soon."

Nicole stepped into her bath, puckered her lips, and smacked them twice, sending kisses through the phone before switching it off. Resting against the tub, she gathered her hair at the top of her head, twisted it into a bun, and looked to her left at the teak wood-paneled wall. She was glad she'd insisted on having a window installed over the tub when she remodeled the house.

A stream of lightning flashes behind distant cotton-ball clouds caught her attention as they took on a bluish-purple hue.

Her eyes closed as she inhaled the peony fragrance diffusing from her bath. She turned away from the window, hoping for a heavy downpour. The continuous patter of rain on the roof was hypnotic and would make for a good night's sleep.

She sighed at the realization that she'd forgotten to switch on music. *It's not going to happen now. That's for sure. I'm already too comfortable to move.* A chuckle escaped her as she remembered what happened the last time. After switching on what she had thought was smooth jazz, she'd leaned back against the tub and closed her eyes. Ten seconds into the instrumental, her eyes had sprung open as timpani drums pounded hard and fast over French horns and violins and climbed to a climactic end. The epic soundtrack had caused her to envision chariots racing toward each other as gladiators wielded swords in battle.

Relaxing bath ruined.

Only me, she thought, shaking her head.

She lifted her bubble-engulfed hand and gently blew the foam away from her.

A crashing sound caused her to sit up. Her eyes focused on a blank spot on the wall as she listened for another minute. All was silent except for the sound of tiny bubbles popping in her bath.

Suddenly, something slammed into the wall behind her.

She sprang up, sloshing water across the tiled floor, and threw on the first thing she could find while still sopping wet. Without thinking, she grabbed the shotgun she kept next to the bed in the adjoining room, and on her tiptoes, slowly made her way to the locked bedroom door. She placed her ear close to the frame and listened before carefully removing the two-by-four barricade that rested in brackets across the middle of the door.

Her hand shook as she reached for the knob. She held her breath and cracked the door open enough to peek into the hall, hoping the hinges wouldn't squeak.

Something ran by.

Nicole gasped and shut the door, locking it again.

Nails scraped against the floor, clawing down the hallway, charging at the door. The thing let out a bloodthirsty growl.

Nicole cried out with each impact as she fumbled with the barricade, attempting to reinstall it.

There's no way out of here, she thought, glancing around the room. The window wasn't an option. It was too far of a fall.

Is this how it ends? What about my baby?

They were never safe. It was foolish of her to think they were.

No one would ever be safe again.

What will the reports show? Wife and mother found mauled to death? She looked back at the door. It was cracking, splinters forming—pushing inward. The creature would be through it with the next ram.

Tears ran down her face as she aimed the shotgun at the door. "Oh God, oh God," she whispered as she slid down the wall to the floor.

She couldn't catch her breath. *This is my fate. I caused this.* Her heart raced as she turned the shotgun away from the door and aimed it at herself, placing the barrel under her chin. She closed her eyes and held her breath, her finger inching toward the trigger.

In her fright, she hadn't noticed that the growling had stopped.

The doorknob jostled, followed by a gentle knock on the door.

"Mommy, I had a bad dream. Mommy, why is your door locked?"

Nicole's eyes flashed open.

CHAPTER 2

*T*welve Years Later

"Get your story straight," Aiden mumbled before stepping in front of his condo door. "Am I going to lie? Of course not. That's not the kind of relationship we have. There are no secrets between us." He grinned slyly. "I'm just going to maneuver my way around the conversation. I got this."

Aiden placed his hand on the BioScan entry key, and the door slid open. "Mom, I'm home!"

"Welcome home, Aiden. May I announce you?"

"No, Tab. I just did. She knows I'm here."

He dropped his sack of books on the bench in the foyer as the front door slid shut behind him. To his left, birds chirped in the three-dimensional display of a Japanese garden oasis. The audio was so crisp and the image so clear that he could've stepped into another world and time—and just maybe, if he reached his hand forward, he could touch the stream leading to the fountain and smell the blossoms on the trees, which was really the air freshener his mom used to complement the scene.

"Please remember to remove your shoes, Aiden."

He rolled his eyes, sat on the bench, and took each shoe off, dropping it on the floor. "Okay?"

"Thank you, Aiden."

I really don't know why we need this home assistant bot. He shook his head and rubbed his hand through his hair, releasing the ebony strands from their gelled prison. His hair hung loosely around his face as he walked into the open kitchen.

"Mom!"

"I'm coming, Aiden," she responded from the back of the house.

There it was. The voice that was everything to him. English with a hint of a Spanish accent—thicker when she got upset. Even when he had a dream that God spoke to him, God spoke with her voice.

"Didn't you hear me calling you?"

"Aiden Gonzales Quinn, is that the way you greet your mother? Of course, I heard you, *mijo*, but can I pee in peace?" She grabbed his face, kissed him on the cheek, and rubbed his back as she passed. "I didn't wash my hands."

"Yuck, Mom," he exclaimed, running to the sink.

"I'm kidding, I'm kidding." She looked back at him with a questioning expression. "*¿Qué, qué?* What did you want?" She walked to the back wall of cabinets and passed her palm over a screen that delivered the day's mail.

"I—uh. . ."

"Just like I thought. You like calling me. You didn't want anything at all. I'm just a habit for you," she said as she faked crying. "You've been antiquing, I see. That's why you're so late getting home, huh?"

Aiden averted his eyes. *Don't look away. Smile, stupid. You know the smile gets her every time.*

He smiled and walked toward his mother, kissed her on the cheek, and rested his head on her shoulder. "I love you, Mommy."

"Yeah, I bet you do."

Without notice, she twisted her body to the left, away from him, causing him to fall off balance as his head dropped from her shoulder. "Let's see what you've got here." She reached for his books. Her eyebrows raised, then furrowed while reading the titles aloud. "No and no."

"But Mom—"

"Moby Dick? Are you serious? Sorry, not happening, *mijo.*" She tossed the book on the counter and went back to the mail. "Hey, look at this. *Ven aquí. Dios mío.*"

"What is it? What's wrong?" He watched her face. She didn't look frightened or angry. Her eyes filled with excitement as she tried not to grin. Aiden may have looked a lot like his father, but his eyes and smile were hers. Her eyes brightened as she read. *It's good news.*

"You got in! You're invited to attend the Institute for Special Minds."

"That's not what it's called. What does it say?"

"You read it," she said while smacking him on the bottom. "I'm pretty sure you were calling me about food, and nothing but food, so help you God. So let me get to it."

Aiden shook his head. *Why does she have to be an attorney?* He tapped the audio tab.

Dear Mr. Quinn,

Thank you for your submission. After careful study of your application and credentials, we would like to offer you an invitation to attend courses at the Institute of Anomalous Intelligence.

As you know, the Institute of Anomalous Intelligence is an organization providing advanced courses of study in science and technology for those who have shown exceptional abilities in these areas. Our courses also count as college credit and will apply to your future academics.

We are only accepting a limited number of students. We hope to see you next week at orientation. Admittance is immediate.

Sincerely,

Dr. Kenneth Laribe, Dean of Students

"I can't believe they've chosen me."

"Well, you are at the top of your class, and I don't think you even study. If I went to school year-round like you guys, maybe I would've had those kinds of grades too."

"Yeah, uh huh." Aiden ran through the great room and down the hall to his bedroom, dodging furniture along the way and ignoring the pulse of pain that shot up his leg from hitting the corner of the coffee table in passing. "Call me when dinner is ready!"

He waved his hand over his desk, and his CPU-bot greeted him in a female voice that sounded more human than robotic—his latest attempt at vocalizing his bot.

"Welcome home. How was your day, Aiden? What may I assist you with?"

"Make sure the chamber is charged," his mother yelled after him.

Why does she always yell? That's what we have Tab for.

He knew why she yelled. Payback. He had just done the same thing to her when he arrived.

"Okay, and FYI, I would prefer a margarita with dinner tonight instead of wine."

"Oh, I'm the parent who gives her son liquor now? Oops, my bad. Sure, whatever you say."

CHAPTER 3

A iden's bedroom was his sanctuary, his favorite room in the house. He walked toward his sleep chamber, passing his fifty-gallon fish tank filled with cichlids, and backed up. He grabbed the yellow tube of fish food from the top of the tank, popped the lid off, and watched his fish. "Sorry, guys. I've been neglecting you."

The oscars saw him first and swam toward the top of the tank. *Greedy.* He dropped chunks of food into the water and watched them. Othello, his albino oscar, raced up, dominating the meal.

The mated pink convicts were the last to come out from under their dwelling, pieces of broken clay pots. They bred and were trying to protect the few fry left, as the other cichlids had devoured them. It had almost brought Aiden to tears. It was his fault. He had been lazy about moving them to another tank.

He waited for the pink convicts to come up through the floating plants on the left side of the tank and placed food there.

"Don't worry, I'll take better care of you."

A couple of oscars swam over but came to a stop, having reached the glass partition Aiden placed in the tank, separating them.

Aiden deepened his voice and spoke with an English accent while yanking his wooden sword from its hook on the wall. Arms raised, he turned full circle around the large room. "Inhabitants of Middle-ocean, your human king has returned. I am victorious. There is peace once again in Middle-ocean."

He laughed, closed the lid of the tank, and slid the panel above it shut.

Oh yeah, the chamber. He knelt below the seven-foot-long capsule, listening for the slight hum of the motor. On top, green bars lit up straight across the panel. "Yep, charged as always. The planet should be safe tonight.

"Show me all the information you have on the Institute of Anomalous Intelligence," he instructed his CPU-bot.

"Certainly."

A hologram of the campus appeared over his desk and slowly rotated, revealing every angle of the structure and the grounds as the CPU-bot spoke. He had seen it all before, but this time was different. He really studied it. "Wait, are those real trees and real grass, or just a mock-up?"

"It appears they are real."

Aiden listened to the rest of the information but quickly became bored with the extra details. He sniffed the air. Whatever his mother was cooking wafted down the hall. His stomach growled.

"Aiden. Food. Come. *Ahora!*"

Sheesh, still not using her home-assistant bot.

"Ha! Ha! I was like, don't make me throat-punch you."

Aiden shook his head. His mother was sometimes loud when on a call with a girlfriend. There was no question she was venting about one of her clients. That meant he could take a little time to find out more about the Institute. *Dinner convo should be interesting tonight.*

He stepped into his en suite and splashed water on his face as the local news and his social media feeds ran down the right side of his mirror.

"What about sports?" he asked as he ran cold water over a towel.

"Stand by."

He held the cool, damp towel over his eyes, still feeling the residual pangs of the migraine he'd had earlier. They were becoming more frequent, but he'd decided against telling his mother about them. She would ask about his medication—the medication he'd stopped taking.

"Shall I send the information to your en suite?"

"No." Aiden dried his face and walked back to his desk.

The hologram expanded on one image after another—tennis courts, a track and football field, and a swimming pool a mile behind the rec center. "The Institute's athletics teams compete against the best of high school and junior college teams."

"Wow," Aiden responded. "No one has outdoor events."

The bot continued reading as Aiden headed for the door. "Stop. Repeat," he said as his steps slowed.

"The facility has a hall of residence, and each student has his own suite."

Aiden turned to face the hologram. *I've never read that before.* "You mean it has a dormitory?"

"That is correct."

"That's huge. It looks like an apartment building. Well, there goes that," he sighed and clenched his hands together. "Mom will never go for it."

"Sleep mode," he instructed the bot before leaving. The images dissolved, and the room darkened behind him. As he turned into the hall, a light flashed on and off.

Aiden backed up and stared at his desk. *That's weird. What blinked?* He waited, walked away, and then popped back through the doorway, but didn't see it happen again.

"*Darse prisa,*" Mrs. Quinn yelled, telling him to hurry up.

CHAPTER 4

1 *0 pm*

Aiden watched his best friend via the clear display monitor over his desk. "Coult, what are you going to do? Are you going to the game or not?"

"You act like I have a choice."

"You know she'll be there, sitting with her marching band drill squad. Take her to the side and tell her you love her and that you don't want to live without her, or whatever you've filled her head with, so you can get back in her good graces."

"You talk to her for me. Be my wingman."

"That I am, but nah, I'm not getting involved in your relationship issues. I tried to tell you to leave that girl alone when you insisted I introduce you two at youth group. She's crazy, her momma's crazy—don't look at me like that. I don't care that they go to my church. It's true. Now, look at you. She's on your mind all day, interfering with everything you do. You're following behind her like you've lost your mind. Just pitiful. I feel like slapping you right now."

"You wouldn't slap a flea."

"Ha! I know, right?"

"Dude, help me. You're my spirit animal."

"Your spirit—" Aiden couldn't stop laughing. "That right there was the absolute best." Aiden's eyes darted back and forth in front of him as he spoke.

"Yeah, I don't know where that came from." Coulter laughed. "What are you looking at? Are you typing?"

"Yeah."

"Anyway, none of what you said is true."

"Yes, it is. What's that old term they used to say? Oh yeah, you're sprung."

"Whatever. Thanks for helping me figure it out," Coulter replied sarcastically.

10:30 pm

"Aiden, are you in bed?"

"What? No. Mom, why are you always yelling?"

"Does your mommy always check on her baby?" Coulter teased.

"Shut it."

"Did you finish your paper?"

"Just did, while we were talking."

"And you'll still walk away with an A. Must be nice. While the rest of us must study and put forth an effort, you walk through this stuff in your sleep."

"Thanks, bro. It's very kind of you to praise me for having the highest GPA in the academy."

"Here we go."

"I'll remember you during my valedictorian speech next year."

"Speaking of speeches, when are you going to talk to you-know-who?"

"Never. She's not interested . . . she's not."

"Look, I'm going to tell you something I've noticed but have never mentioned to you."

"I'm listening."

"You are as blind as a bat."

"That phrase is inaccurate. Bats can see as well as humans. They use echolocation at night, though."

Coulter stared at Aiden with a straight face. "What. Ever. You're deaf, too. Girls are always watching you."

"No, they aren't."

"They do, but you never notice. And I've heard them." Coulter mimicked a girl's voice. "'I want his hair. His eyes give me life. He's rich. He's so sweet.' Yet you see and hear none of this because you're walking around in this 'pity me' bubble, and I don't have a clue why."

Aiden stared at the screen. "You're not wearing glasses."

"Are you telling me you're just noticing I'm not wearing glasses after two years? No, I know what you're doing."

"What am I doing?"

"You're trying to change the subject like the punk you are."

"Isn't it nice that we are such good friends we can call each other names and insult each other and not get upset?"

"Okay, I'm disconnecting."

"May God bless and keep you and strengthen you with power and might to go and make up with crazy Liv."

The screen went black.

11:00 pm

Aiden lay in his chamber thinking and biting at a hangnail. *How will the Institute deal with my being a—it won't work. Why did I allow myself to get my hopes up?*

11:30 pm

Mrs. Quinn entered Aiden's room and found him asleep in his chamber. She checked the readings and made a mental note that his oxygen supply levels were getting a little low. Turning to leave the room, she tossed his clothes into his hamper and stopped just outside the door to set her wristband for one o'clock.

"Tab?"

"Yes, Mrs. Quinn?"

"Secure the house."

"Yes, Mrs. Quinn."

The thud of vault doors sealing off each room as she passed brought little comfort. Everything depended on what was going on in Aiden's mind.

Once inside her bedroom, a steel panel locked in place behind her door. She yawned as she removed her robe and sat on the side of her bed in her pajama pants and tank top. She unlocked her bedside table with her iris scan, removed her pistol from the drawer and placed it, along with her combat knife, under the pillow next to her.

12:45 am
"Mrs. Quinn? Mrs. Quinn?"
She awoke and sat up. "Yes, Tab?"
"It has begun."

CHAPTER 5

Mrs. Quinn rubbed her eyes to make sure she wasn't seeing things. The walls were pulsating.

She leaned back against her pillows and tapped one of the buttons on the holoboard beside her as she yawned. Six images of areas around the home appeared in front of her. She tapped again, and six other areas appeared.

"Do you see him, Mrs. Quinn?"

"Yes, I do, Tab. Is he human or an entity?"

"I detect neither, Mrs. Quinn."

"Neither? What does that mean, T—"

"Shall I implement disposal procedures?"

"Not yet. He doesn't seem to be doing anything except looking."

Something that looked like a man walked down the hall, checking doors. Unable to get inside, he pounded on the doors with his fists. Each blow emitted a red spark upon contact. He groaned in anger and turned, eyeing the door behind him.

"He's heading for Aiden's room. Tab, unlock the hatch."

He ran his hands over the door and along the edges.

"He's trying to find a way in. Okay, it's time to handle this."

Mrs. Quinn reached under the pillow for her knife and pistol and placed them in the holster she wore. She was calm. There was nothing she hadn't seen during one of these manifestations. Aiden would be fine. She was sure of that, but she needed to hurry before things got out of hand. That was the key, waking him as quickly as possible.

She approached her closet as the floor access hatch opened, and a ladder extended down into Aiden's closet.

"Mrs. Quinn, wait."

"There's no time, Tab."

She climbed down, and as she exited into his en suite, her wrist alarm went off. *Crap, I forgot.*

She stopped in her tracks. Two women stood between her and Aiden. They'd been staring down into the glass lid of his chamber. They turned, hearing the ringing behind them.

Mrs. Quinn walked toward them, pointing her pistol back and forth between them.

They stepped together, backing away.

She glanced toward the door, hearing the man pounding on the other side. The door, reinforced with concrete and steel, shook with each blow.

She backed toward Aiden's sleep chamber without taking her eyes off the women.

The pounding on the door stopped.

Something's behind me, she thought. She couldn't see anything, but she felt a presence. "Tab, wake—"

Hands reached around her. A hot, callused hand covered her mouth, and another grabbed at her arm, pulling for the pistol. It was the man that had been outside the door. She was sure of it.

The women rushed forward. A fist slammed across her jaw, sending a pulse through the side of her head. She grimaced. *Don't lose consciousness, Nikki. You can't black out.* It was her voice, but it wasn't her saying it.

She released one hand from the pistol and allowed the women to push her against the man so she could reach back toward Aiden's chamber.

The man pulled her to the side. She groaned and strained to angle her body toward the chamber. Her hand inched across the panel until the tip of her finger pushed a button.

A pulse tore through the mattress and lifted Aiden up and back down. Aiden's eyes shot open. The lid of the sleep chamber lifted, and he sat up.

He looked down at the pistol now at his mother's side. "Mom, what happened? Your jaw is red. Are you okay?"

She breathed heavily. "I'm fine."

Aiden leaped over the side of the chamber, looking around the room.

"Were you injured?"

"Aiden, I told you I'm fine."

His voice shook. "I'm so sorry. I'm sick of this. Are you really okay?"

She smiled at him. "I'm absolutely okay. What do I always say? Huh?"

They said it together. "All in a day's work."

"Come with me, *mijo*."

Aiden hugged her, and they walked over to his sitting area. "Tab, music, please."

Soft music filled the room. She laid her back against the sofa, still breathing heavily.

"Did I cause any damage? Was this a bad one?"

"Not at all. A piece of cake compared to what we've experienced in the past."

He looked at her in disbelief.

"Aiden, I've fought werewolves, vampires, and ninjas to get to you. I have the scars to show for it. This was nothing, okay? I wouldn't lie about it."

Aiden nodded. He looked down at his lap. "I've done things I wish I could take back, but I can't. I can't even stop what's happening. What good is the sleep chamber if it doesn't help control my sleep-induced state? Isn't the medi-mist it sprays supposed to help?"

"It *is* helping. There have been fewer manifestations than in the past."

"It's not enough. I don't want your life at risk."

"Playback, Tab."

"Yes, Mrs. Quinn."

She folded her legs under her and pointed at the display wall. "Tell me about the man with the towel around his neck."

"I saw him in the hall today."

"On our floor?"

"No, on the third lobby level."

"What do you think made you dream about him?"

"I don't know. I think I saw him earlier when I got off the travelator. He followed me. If it wasn't him, they looked alike."

"How much alike?"

"Exactly alike. He was weird. He stared at me but didn't speak."

"You spoke to him, and he said nothing back?"

"Not a word."

"That *is* weird. What about the two women?"

"They were on the elevator. It was the same type of deal. They just stared at me when I got off. I really didn't think much about either encounter."

"Yeah, but it affected you in a deeper place—in your warning zone."

"Warning zone?"

She tapped her chest. "You know, that place deep inside that gives us warnings—something told me to do this, or something told me it was you."

"Oh, I guess so."

"I'm going to up the security around here."

"I don't think that's necessary."

"This is not even up for discussion. You know I go with my instincts."

"Your warning zone."

"Exactly. I need to ice this face. Warm milk?" she asked as she stood.

Aiden nodded. "Since I'm up."

"And why would you dream the woman's skirt in her crack?" She laughed and grabbed her jaw. *Ow!*

"That's how she was on the elevator."

"Really? See, all of this is why I'm not so sure about you going off to school. What if you have a manifestation there?"

"Mom, I can't live like this my whole life. People are going to find out about me. I've come to terms with it. I've read every report after the fifty million tests ran on me. I'm the only person like this in the world. I get it.

"A Canadian scientist discovered the mutation five years ago, and I'm what they've termed a Sleeper. Woo-hoo, I have a category now," he added sarcastically. "It's time for the world to know that a real-life mutant lives among them."

"Mutant? Kid, you need to stop it."

CHAPTER 6

❯❯ I don't know how I allowed you to talk me into this," Mrs. Quinn fussed as she pulled her mass of dark curls together and tied a band around them.

Aiden watched her. She'd told him people took her seriously with her hair pulled back. She never appeared in court with it down. That meant she was shifting into attorney mode. *God help us.*

"We are just going to have a look around and then decide from there. That was our agreement, right? Painless," he replied.

He ignored her side-eye as they waited to board the Teslaloop. A gush of wind and the rumble of the platform beneath their feet announced the approach of the elevated steel tube.

The Teslaloop glided forward and came to a stop in front of them. Several passengers exited on the opposite side before their door opened. Aiden and Mrs. Quinn entered and sat at the back, facing forward.

Aiden watched the few other people in the capsule. A man stared out the window, seemingly unaware of anyone else, his shoulders hunched and head hanging low, almost touching the window. A woman held a tissue to her nose as she studied something on her tablet. An impeccably dressed man and woman leaned toward each other, engrossed in conversation. A woman stood against the wall, a sack between her feet, eyes heavy. *Five. Four. Three. Two . . . and she's asleep.*

Aiden smiled to himself. Surely, they weren't as fortunate as he—accepted to the school of his dreams and headed there now. The heel of his foot tapped incessantly because of his anxiety. He turned his head away from his mother and grinned. He didn't want her to detect how siced he was.

Within thirty minutes, they arrived at their stop, and as soon as they stepped out of the station, Aiden had a bizarre feeling.

I belong here.

The air felt different, fresher, better. He inhaled deeply and looked around. He could see the Institute of Anomalous Intelligence from the elevated platform. *It's actually on the ground.*

Aiden turned to his mother with a grin. "We've gone back in time."

Instead of a modern structure, they looked out over the grounds of a huge castle-like building making up the front of the property. A tall fence surrounded the land, and its gate remained open for the festivities of the day. Red letters outlined in white read *WELCOME* over the blue banner that hung from the gate. As they approached the building, a ten-foot stone wall matching the stone on the exterior of the building cut off the entrance.

They stood for a moment, admiring the structure. "What do you think?" asked Aiden.

"Hmph, mediocre."

"Ha! Nice try, Mom. There is nothing mediocre about this place." He placed his arms around her, picking her up in the air.

She chuckled as he swung her around. "I told you about doing that. Put me down. Let's try to appear civilized."

Stairs led up either side of a fountain built into the stone wall. "They are making us get our exercise today," she stated before climbing the stairs.

Aiden didn't care. He was too busy taking in the smell of the evergreens. His feet crunched over small brown leaves that covered the lawn. He stared at the blades of grass, wishing he could kneel and smell them, put his fingers in the soil, and dig for worms. *Real grass.*

There was one main entrance at the front of the building. Two wide steps led up to the front door. Aiden ran his hand over the leaves of the round topiaries on either side.

An enthusiastic student aide met them at the door. "Hello, my name is Trude, and I am your orientation leader. Welcome to the Institute of Anomalous Intelligence." She held out her hand.

Aiden tapped the back of his fist to hers.

Mrs. Quinn nodded toward her.

"I'm going to take you on a tour of this magnificent campus and then lead you back to the Dean's conference for any questions you may have. Excellent? Excellent," she responded to herself, turned, and started down the corridor.

Aiden and Mrs. Quinn looked at each other. "I guess we're supposed to follow her," his mother said.

"Yeah, hurry. She's like running the sixty-yard dash."

"I hope the tour goes just as quickly," she quipped.

Aiden took his mother's hand and pulled. "Come on, counselor. Please turn off your detective radar for now."

As they walked, Trude informed them that the Institute expected the students to act as adults. "There are no chaperones. All incoming high school students are treated as college freshmen. I'm sure you remember that one of your requirements for the program was that you test at freshman level or higher."

Aiden's mother shot him a glance.

"Oh boy, here we go," he thought.

"I don't think you're ready for that. You're still a kid."

"No, I am not," he grunted.

They toured all the campus buildings and admired the acres of grounds. Trude pointed out an interesting fact about the outside walls of the classrooms. Those in the hall could see through them, but the students couldn't see out.

"No distractions."

Students passed by here and there on their way to the dorm, eatery, or rec center. They were friendly and open to questions. Some of them floated by on hoverboards.

One student saw them watching. He smiled and waved. "It's a large campus. This makes it easier." He was a pro at it. He rode through the air to the side like he was surfing on wind.

Aiden watched a girl running to catch her friend. "Helena," she called. "Are you coming? We're playing airball. I added you to our team." The other girl jogged after her, grinning.

"Well, she seems excited. What's airball?" asked Mrs. Quinn.

"It's kind of like football and volleyball combined, but you wear boots that keep you a few feet off the ground by moving air with electromagnetic fields."

"Interesting. Why have I never heard of this?"

"You don't even like sports."

"You may join their game if you like," Trude offered.

"That's okay, he won't have time for that. We'll be leaving soon," Mrs. Quinn responded.

Aiden grimaced and held his fingers against his temples.

"What is it? A migraine?"

Leave. Leave now. Aiden heard his own voice in his head telling him this, but it wasn't him. *Leave? Why am I thinking that?*

The pain subsided quickly. "No, I'm okay."

"Look at me."

Aiden looked into his mother's eyes. "See? I'm okay. Can we continue now?"

CHAPTER 7

"**P**arents, it is now time to separate you from the students so you may freely ask all the questions you have or inform us of any concerns," Trude announced. "We will meet in the conference room along with some of the professors that will be instructing your children. There, you will also meet the Dean of Students, Dr. Laribe.

"Students, you may remain here. When you're new, it's nice to see a familiar face on campus. I suggest you use this time to get to know one another.

"This way, please," Trude instructed the parents.

Mrs. Quinn turned to Aiden with an irritated expression as Trude ushered her out.

He clasped his hands together and responded with a look that pleaded with her to cooperate.

As soon as the last parent left, Aiden turned to face the room. Most of the students stood around, staring. *Well, if no one wants to talk, I might as well eat something. Do they realize I can see them watching me?*

Aiden studied the architecture of the room as he walked toward the buffet table. Hardwood floors, wainscoting covering the lower portion of the walls, and huge wood-framed windows.

They were in the main building of the campus, the administrative one, which was a remodeled mansion.

He looked over the display of desserts, fruits, and vegetables. *I'm too anxious to eat any of this. Maybe a cube of cheese,* he thought as someone approached him.

"I'm Lax. Lax Petropoulos."

The introduction came from a tall dark-haired boy.

"My family is in engine manufacturing. I'm into football but they're against it, so I'll probably become a mechanical engineer. Don't eat that." He hit Aiden's hand, and the cheese to dropped to the floor. "Try this instead." He handed Aiden a cube of cheese infused with fruit as he tossed one into his mouth.

Aiden stared at the cheese. *He just touched it.*

"Go ahead," said Lax.

Aiden shrugged, silently prayed that any contamination from the boy's hand miraculously dissolved, and willed himself to chew.

An explosion of flavor went off in his mouth. He nodded as he enjoyed the taste of a sweet red Comice pear swirling around a creamy sharp cheese. He didn't even realize he was smiling.

Lax grinned. "See, I told you. No one eats that other stuff anymore. I don't even know why they have it here, a big operation such as this. Is that prosciutto? Don't eat it, it may be raw. Whoa, look at that cuteness. So how did you like your tour guide?"

"What?" Aiden swallowed while trying to take in everything the immediately-likable speed talker had said.

"She wasn't real."

"But we pressed hands," said Aiden.

"I know. She's a sim. Impressive, right?"

"Wow."

"Yeah, they could make a whole city of them, and no one would be the wiser."

"How did you know?"

"Oh, I'm already a student here. They let me in on the inner workings of things. You know, all the important stuff. They say I have a mind for it." He blew on his fist and polished it on his chest. He then flicked his collar up.

Where have I seen those gestures? Some old movie, I think, thought Aiden.

Another kid, Ellison, or Fitz as he preferred to be called, approached them. He had bushy eyebrows that were almost connecting in the center. "Hey, how do you get away with wearing your hair that long at school? Are you homeschooled?"

"No. Not yet, anyway. I gel it back for school."

"But still, it's long and goes against school policy," another kid added. "I'm Quest."

"Aiden. I insist on having my own identity. I refuse to be a clone." *Why is my hair the topic of conversation? Funny.*

"Clones are against the law," the cute girl Lax had referred to said while walking up to them. She stopped in front of Aiden.

"And yet, they are still engineering them," Aiden responded, looking her in the eye. *She's not looking away.* He flinched. Cupid shot him—again.

Lax looked back and forth between them. "Oh crap, he's going *Gatsby* on us."

"Is that a thing?" asked Quest.

"Yeah," Fitz chimed in and pointed. "He's Gatsby, she's Daisy."

Quest nodded in understanding. "Ooooooh." *The Great Gatsby* had been a part of every high school Advanced Literature course.

Lax waved his hand in front of Aiden's face. Aiden didn't blink. "Dude, you've known her for all of two seconds."

"I can spot a clone a mile away," another kid said, entering the conversation.

"You're staring," the girl stated.

"No, *you're* staring," Aiden replied. "I'm just staring back to prove I'm not a punk. If I look away first, I lose."

Lax smirked and shook his head.

She grinned. "I'm Danai."

"I'm Aiden."

"I'm not even here," said the last kid.

"Sorry, man," Aiden replied. He held the back of his fist at the kid, who then bumped it.

He was younger than the rest and a genius. He introduced himself as Halland.

"Hey, Hal," said Lax.

"What about that girl over there? Does anyone know her?" Aiden pointed at a girl near the window. The gray under her puffy eyes stood out against her pale skin. "She looks like she hasn't slept in weeks."

She sat on the windowsill looking out at the front lawn and lifted the hood of her grey sweater over her head. She then crossed her arms in front of her as if she were cold.

"I don't think she wants to be bothered."

Lax waved at her. "Heyyyyyy, helloooooooo."

She ignored everyone while Aiden and his new friends joined another group that had formed on the other side of the room. He didn't know how he would remember all their names—other than Danai.

The other group consisted of Perch, her hair cut short, pixie style, and she wore glasses; Stern, another big guy, but nowhere as friendly as Lax; Tristan, Aiden wondered about the scars on his wrists; Bale, he came from a military school; and Oui, who could build his own supercomputer.

As everyone listened to Quest, who was caught up in the moment and unable to talk about anything but dimensional travel, Aiden looked back at the girl who sat at the window, occasionally glancing over at them.

There's something familiar about her.

CHAPTER 8

*T*his is what it feels like to be popular, thought Aiden.

Everyone in the room had made a point to talk to him and get to know him. *Enjoy it while you can. Soon enough they will all find you weird and distance themselves.*

"Hey, come here," said Lax.

He introduced Aiden to a few other students who peeked in just to see what was happening. They were eager to raid the buffet table that the orientation attendees ignored.

Aiden watched the body language of one of the students, a female with thick, dark hair and heavy bangs. She seemed enamored with Lax. Why wouldn't she be? He was the ideal athlete. The captain of the football team, most popular guy in school, homecoming king type. Except he wasn't arrogant or rude, which was what kept Aiden from calling him a jock.

An hour later, Trude reappeared with their parents. A man walked between them. He was six feet tall, had a muscular build, and looked to be about fiftyish years old.

Trude introduced them. "Dr. Laribe, this is Aiden Quinn."

He turned to Aiden. "I know exactly who this is. I am so *very* pleased to meet you, Mr. Quinn. You, my friend, are extremely impressive. A natural-born leader." He leaned toward Aiden's ear and lowered his voice. "I'm glad we could get to you before you accepted that early enrollment at MIT."

How did he know about that? Aiden thought. He looked over at his mother as she stepped to his side. He hadn't told her he'd applied to the Massachusetts Institute of Technology, and he was glad Dr. Laribe had whispered the information.

"I understand your focus of study is in Chemistry and Brain and Cognitive Sciences."

"Yes, sir. That's correct."

"You will do well here. There's a lab I would love to get your feedback on after you begin classes."

"Yes, of course," Aiden said with enthusiasm. "That would be great, sir."

Aiden moved out of the way and watched as Dr. Laribe greeted the other students. He marveled at how Dr. Laribe knew so much about each one of them and mentioned aspects of their essays or studies that had impressed him. He had an infectious smile and was the most approachable person Aiden had ever met.

Aiden made up his mind. *I want this—all of it. I want to experience campus life and finally have classes advanced enough to study for.* He just needed his mother to be okay with it.

Despite Mrs. Quinn's eagerness to end the tour, they were one of the last families to leave. Aiden waved goodbye to some of his new friends and looked over at how his mother had Dr. Laribe cornered. He shook his head. *She's interrogating him.*

Other parents joined the conversation, nodding, appreciating the extra questions she'd come up with. Aiden had to admit, the dean was being a good sport and didn't seem to mind. At least he had answers for her.

Mrs. Quinn whispered something in Dr. Laribe's ear. The dean looked shocked, but then a smile crept over his face. He nodded in understanding, but Aiden was sure he could see a hint of annoyance. *She's aggravating him. But if I pull her away, she'll be on my case for the rest of the night for interfering. It's best to let her do what she does.*

He looked out the window, seeing the girl in the grey sweater headed toward the Teslaloop station. She looked toward the building in his direction. He wasn't sure if she could see him, but the way she looked up jogged a memory.

That's it! I know her! She looked at me the same way back then. "Mom, I'll be right back," Aiden whispered while dashing past her.

"Where are you—"

Aiden ran down the stairs and out the front door of the building. "Hey!" *What's her name? Famia? Farmasia? Think!* "Farmer!"

Farmer stopped and looked over her shoulder. *That's it! Sometimes I amaze myself.*

He couldn't tell if she remembered him or not. She looked exhausted, but even so, he noticed how unique her eyes were. The outer corners slanted up, and she had long chestnut lashes.

He walked toward her and spoke gently and carefully. "You probably don't remember me . . . from Canada?"

She watched him but did not answer. Her face showed no emotion.

Okay, she is not going to make this easy, but if my assumption is right . . . "Listen, sometimes I have trouble sleeping. May I share with you what helps?"

Farmer didn't respond.

Hello, is anyone in there? Aiden cleared his throat. "While you're getting ready for bed, listen to calming music or watch a funny movie. Think only about things that make you happy before you drift off to sleep. Begin this an hour or two before bed and be careful of what you allow in your head throughout the day. Your own thoughts can be your worst enemy, so don't dwell on negative things. Trust me, it works. It will help you sleep. He smiled, but Farmer didn't smile back. She looked confused, then she turned and ran to catch up with her parents.

That was stupid. Why did I just do that? He tapped his forehead with the palm of his hand. *I sound like a real nut job. I put myself out there and . . .* He watched Farmer's arm movement as she walked.

She tapped her wrist.

She recorded it, he thought, smiling to himself.

"What was that about?" Mrs. Quinn asked, joining him outside. "Are you trying to get her number?"

"Seriously, Mom? Girls don't notice me. Coulter claims they do, but I don't believe him. Their mothers and grandmothers notice me. 'Oh, he's so cute, look at his hair.' Blah blah blah. Why is that?"

Mrs. Quinn giggled. "That was cute the way you mimicked an old woman's voice. Anyway, they can see what you will become."

"I'm not attractive now?"

"You are. If you were ugly, I would tell you and you know it. I would say something like, 'Son, you're not an appreciated type of handsome, so you'll have to make up for it with your personality and smarts.' But I don't have to say anything like that, because you have it all."

"Then why don't they notice?"

"Because girls are stupid at your age. And you know what else?"

Oh no, why did I start this?

"One will show no interest in you, and then as soon as she sees someone else is interested, here she'll come. When that happens, and it will happen," she said while pointing at him, "you better not go back to the one who ignored you. Trust. The right one will notice you from the start, and—"

"Mom. Mom!" he spoke over her. "Okay, I got it."

"So what did you run after her for, anyway?"

"That was Farmer. Remember? From the Neurological Institute in Canada a few years ago? We were there being tested in the sleep disorders department at the same time."

"Yeah, yeah, right. She was in foster care, right? Were those her parents?"

"I don't know."

"Small world."

"I told her some things to try to help her sleep."

"She's not sleeping?"

"I don't think so. Maybe she's not able to get help."

"Not everyone is as fortunate as you. Remember that," Mrs. Quinn said while wrapping an arm around Aiden's shoulder.

"Not everyone is fortunate to have one of the top attorneys in the country as a mother."

"Flattery will get you everywhere with me, *mijo*."

"So what did you think of—"

"Un-uh. We're not having that conversation tonight. We will sleep on it and discuss it tomorrow."

Aiden knew when not to push the issue. "Pizza?"

"Sheesh. Of course. You should just make it a statement, not a question. When have I ever turned down pizza?"

CHAPTER 9

A iden's viewer switched on and recorded an image of his head bopping up and down as he mimicked the sounds of a drum machine.

His hair fell in thick waves around his face and down to his collar. He looked up, seeing the *record* light flashing.

"Oh, it's on. What's up, good people?" he said in the tone he used when he rapped along to his favorite hip hop song. "I know I seem a little happy. That's because I am."

He tried to jump and click his heels together but failed.

"That was embarrassing, but I'm too pumped to care." Aiden smiled wide, still elated about his acceptance and his mother breaking down and allowing him to attend classes at the Institute of Anomalous Intelligence. Was it because he stopped speaking to her, hardly ate anything, and moped around the house like his world was over? Who knows?

"This will be my last entry for a little while. Unfortunately, the Institute doesn't allow viewers on campus. I think it's because of the research that takes place here. Top secret stuff. Bummer. But you know, they don't mind my hair length, and we don't have to wear a stupid school uniform, so it's cool. I'll begin recording entries again during quarter break.

"Classes start tomorrow. Check it out." The viewer turned, showing a wall of twenty-foot glass windows. Students sat outside on the lawn. A glass wall on the other side of the room allowed students to watch the various games in session.

Aiden placed the viewer on his face again. "I'm in the Zuckerberg Recreational Center and about to get into a game of paddle ball. I've made some new friends. They're different, like me, and *want* to be my friends. This place is like a whole society of nerds. I am right at home here.

"Oh, and there's a girl—again." He thought for a moment. He wasn't sure how much he wanted to say about that. She might see the entry one day. "There's something different about her. Maybe I'll have good news concerning her by the end of the quarter," he said with a wink.

"I haven't met all my instructors yet, but I met Dr. Tussaud and Professor Houser at orientation, and they were okay as teachers go. Houser is younger and maybe more approachable. Oh yeah, speaking of approachable, the Dean of Students, Dr. Laribe, is super cool and really tries to help the students adjust to campus living. He seems genuinely interested in my studies.

"We met this morning and went over my curriculum. He's funny. He tried to be subtle about where I put my focus." Aiden mimicked him. "'I check in on students who I perceive to have the brightest futures. What I don't want to see is a relationship status that reads *in a relationship*, or *it's complicated*. You'll have plenty of time for that later.' Good luck with that one.

"He says I can stop in at his office to talk to him about anything at all. I probably will. My mom always says it's a good idea to have a mentor.

"Well, you guys, I can see Lax coming up the walk, so I'm going to end this now. See you in three months. You probably won't even recognize me because I'm hitting the weights hard. Diesel is what they'll call me," Aiden said with a laugh before switching off the viewer.

He switched it back on. "Don't be jealous. You too can have all of this if you work hard and—"

"Aiden!" yelled Lax. "What are you doing? Why are you talking to yourself?"

CHAPTER 10

"My name is Ms. Genova," the woman standing at the front of the classroom announced. She wore tan slacks and a white blazer buttoned up to the neck. Her long dark hair was parted deeply on the side and pulled back into a low, neat ponytail. As she spoke, her name appeared on the display wall behind her.

"Congratulations. You were all chosen and accepted our invitation to the Institute. However, we administered one final test to ensure you were Anomalous Intelligence material. There are twelve of you in this room. Two of you did not pass the exam and must leave the facility immediately.

"Last night, polysomnographic technologists placed sensors on the head of each student. They monitored you the entire night and took comprehensive recordings of the biophysiological changes that occurred while you slept.

"We use polysomnography to diagnose sleep disorders. The readings of these two students showed their breathing repeatedly stopped and started throughout the night."

She looked around the room as if she were waiting for someone to say something.

"Sleep apnea," Aiden stated.

"Yes, Mr. Quinn. That is correct. We have already contacted the guardians of the students who did not pass, and they are waiting downstairs.

"When I call your name, please come forward."

Aiden suddenly felt as if someone had sucked oxygen from the room.

"Perch Commons."

The name appeared on the wall in red.

Perch, teary-eyed, stood and walked to the front of the room with her head down and took something from Ms. Genova. She looked back over her shoulder and waved goodbye before leaving the room.

The red writing dissolved from the wall.

Aiden's heart beat too fast. *If she doesn't hurry and read the last name, they're going to have a dead kid on their hands.* He placed his hand on his chest. Him being a Sleeper, how could they not have found something wrong with his readings?

"Stern Bleck."

Aiden exhaled.

Stern slammed his fist on the table, rose from his seat, and snatched the slip out of Ms. Genova's hand.

"Security," Ms. Genova stated softly.

Immediately, two guards appeared at the door to escort him out.

The remaining students looked around the room like they had won a group competition. Even Farmer had a slight grin.

"Now, let's move on. I suggest you get to know one another because you will have most of your classes together.

"As you know, the main course of study here is neuroscience, and whether or not you choose to continue your academics in the medical or scientific fields of study, the courses count as college credits. You will administer experiments and take part in them—all in fun.

"You will conduct research for organizations such as the Food and Drug Administration, where you will study recombinant DNA—"

Fitz raised his hand. "What does recombinant DNA have to do with the FDA?"

"Genome editing," Halland whispered.

"That's correct, Mr. Prescott. Do you eat chicken, Mr. Sanka?"

"Yes," Fitz replied.

"Well, along with numerous other things, the FDA studies viruses such as the fowlpox virus in an effort to give us chicken that is unharmed by viruses. In this aspect, they are concerned with the health and welfare of the foods we eat. You will cover this in detail in molecular biology, genetics, and also if you are majoring in biotechnology."

A female bot's voice interrupted the class. *"Room A, proceed to Lab One for your physical exams."*

"You are dismissed," Ms. Genova stated. "Go directly to the lab."

The students rose and followed the hologram site maps, which hovered ahead of them just below the ceiling.

Farmer stopped Aiden outside of the classroom, her voice just above a whisper. "My parents said to thank you for your help."

It surprised Aiden to hear her speak. "What help? Did I help you?" he asked as if he didn't understand what she was talking about.

Farmer laughed. "Yes, you did. How did you know about me?"

"I saw myself in you. There was a time when I had trouble sleeping."

"That too, but how did you know my name?"

"Oh," he laughed. "We met years ago in Canada. Remember? We were being tested for sleep disorders and had to sleep at the lab overnight."

"And you remembered my name?"

"Well, it's a weird name. No, I'm kidding. I remember things. I don't know why. My mom always asks how I know things. Were those your real parents at orientation?"

"No, they adopted me. They adopt kids with special needs. I like it there."

"You're considered special needs?"

"I guess. It's whatever. I don't care what they label me. They understand that I need to be in a loving environment instead of one that invokes fear, like with my fosters. That way, I don't have anxiety and bad dreams about them."

Aiden looked in at the students in the other lecture halls as they passed by them. "They get it."

"Yes. After everything they heard and seeing the reports, they still took me in. That's why I tried not to sleep. I didn't want anything to happen to them."

Aiden's steps slowed. His mind raced as she spoke. *To happen to them?* He studied her. *Why did she say that?*

"Just about anything could trigger a manifestation."

What's happening here? Is she saying that—she can't be—is she saying she's a Sleeper? Say the words. I need to hear you say it.

But Farmer didn't say it. She kept talking as if he already knew about her.

Another Sleeper exists? Okay, okay, pull yourself together. He felt he could jump out of his skin. *Stay cool. Don't act surprised. Act like you hear every day that someone is a Sleeper. Mom is not going to believe this.*

Her arm flew up as she spoke. Bright, glowing beads on her wrist caught his eye. *Those are different. What did she just say? Something about having lived on each city level with her fosters.* He watched her lips. *She's a Sleeper. No, stop going there. Pay attention to what she's saying.*

"My family is very religious. I tried reading the Bible before bed, but that backfired."

Aiden gave a nervous laugh. "Be strategic on what you read from the Bible. Read the book of Psalms, or anything regarding praise. Stay away from the parts about Noah and Samson, and even David." He laughed again. It was too remarkable to believe. He second-guessed himself. *Is that what she's saying? That she's a Sleeper?*

Farmer laughed. "I know. I flooded my house after a Sunday school teaching on Noah's ark." Her laugh, unexpected, genuine, calmed him.

She's a Sleeper.

Aiden watched her blue polished nails comb through her hair as she pulled it back behind her ear. There was something on her neck, just below and behind her earlobe.

"Whoa, wait. Come here."

Farmer pulled back. "What is it? Is it a bug? Get it off me."

"Calm down." He moved closer to her and pulled her hair back. *Her hair is soft.*

"It's in my hair?"

"Shh . . ." He cupped his hands over the area of her neck, peeked inside them at a tiny butterfly, and watched it come to life as it glowed bright blue in the darkness. "You have a tattoo. A neon one at that."

Farmer touched her neck as if she'd just remembered it was there. "Yes, I kind of have a thing for butterflies."

"It's cool."

She averted her eyes. "Thanks. In school, I always had to keep it covered with my hair or makeup. Here, they don't mind our individuality."

"Hence the hair," Aiden said as he pointed at the wavy strands hanging down, covering the left side of his face.

Farmer grasped his arm, stopping him from walking. The warmth of her hand through his shirt made him look down at her. Again, he noticed the glowing beads of her bracelets as she leaned in toward him. She lifted on her toes, kissed him on the cheek, and quickly stepped back.

What was that for? He knew his expression showed what he was thinking.

"Thank you for caring," she said, turned, and walked away.

Aiden stood speechless—still shocked that another Sleeper existed and equally surprised by the kiss. Somewhere deep inside, he was a little excited about both. He wanted another opportunity to talk to her, alone, to leave with her right then. He needed to know everything—did she hate her experiences as a Sleeper as much as he did, if that was why she was orphaned, and everything in between.

CHAPTER 11

A iden's class boarded several elevators with other students. The doors closed behind them, and two seconds later, reopened to a white corridor. Aiden stared out into the hall. "Did anyone feel this thing move?"

Lax shrugged and pushed him. "It had to. You can see we're not on the same floor."

A hologram arrow above their heads directed them to a door at the end of the hall where a man wearing a lab jacket escorted them to a large locker room. "There are gowns in each locker for you to change into," he instructed. "Is there a possibility that any of you are pregnant?"

Fitz and Aiden looked at each other and then at the others. "Surely he means them," Fitz said while motioning toward the girls, who all shook their heads.

The physical was like every other physical Aiden ever had. Two pieces of flat metal hung suspended in the air, one in front of him and the other behind. He stood perfectly still while the scanners lowered to his feet and back up above his head at the same time.

Throughout the physical, Aiden's eyes searched for Farmer. He couldn't seem to stop watching her. *Another Sleeper . . .*

The IQ portion of the exam was last. The students were put through a series of tests they considered nothing more than video games.

"Oh, I've got this," Aiden said as he slid into a chair in front of one of the screens. "This should be fun."

The students were to begin the game at the same time. "Please remember you are not playing against each other, but against yourselves—against your own mind."

"How can you play against your own mind?" Halland whispered to Aiden. "That doesn't make any sense. He has to mean against the computer."

Aiden shrugged.

The screens lit up and BEGIN flashed in front of them.

As soon as they learned a new tool on the game, the game used it against them. Their minds had to work at a fast pace and keep building upon what they learned at the beginning of the game.

The other students became frustrated while trying to finish the second half, the hardest part of the test. Aiden and Halland were the only ones to complete it. It involved using logic to solve a shape-shifting puzzle. The whole thing took an hour to complete.

After the exam, Lax sat on a bench in the locker room, putting on his shoes. "Aiden, where are you headed?"

"Dorm."

"Let's meet up in an hour."

Aiden gave him a thumbs up as he walked out of the locker room, glancing back into the lab for Farmer. The lab was now dark, and everyone was gone. He collapsed back on the wall, his chin dipping to his chest.

As he turned to leave, a flash of light caught his eye. He stepped back into the lab, looking around. The flash was just like the one he'd seen at home in his bedroom. He waited, but it didn't happen again.

Behind him, Lax peeked into the lab. "What's wrong?"

"Did you see that?"

"I see a dark empty room. What did you see?"

"I don't know. Nothing, I guess."

"Don't start getting spooky on me."

"No, it was nothing like that. Just a light."

"Oh. It probably came from one of the monitors. Let's get going."

Aiden nodded but had an uneasy feeling. He remembered his mother's words about his warning zone.

CHAPTER 12

Aiden boarded the SkyTran to the dorm. He'd learned it was the fastest way of getting anywhere on the massive campus. Pod-like cars hung below metal tracks forty feet above the ground and gave the appearance you were floating across to the next building.

The SkyTran let out on the fourth level of the dormitory. The first level housed the residential dining hall, library (essentially a series of computers), and the gaming center. The second and third floors contained the new student dorm suites. Females resided on the second floor and males on the third. Upperclassmen occupied the higher floors.

Aiden hurried and changed clothes so he could meet Lax and Quest in the eatery, another name for the residential dining hall.

"You have a call from Coulter," his CPU-bot stated.

"Connect," Aiden responded. "Visual."

Coulter's face appeared in front of him. "A-bougie, I mean A-boogie, how's it going up there?"

"Not bad so far."

"Yeah, sure."

"No, really. It's no big deal," he lied, not wanting to brag.

"Guess what?"

"Tell me."

"I got wait-listed."

"For the Institute? You applied?" Aiden asked with excitement.

"My best bud left me here with all these sub-normal freaks. What the heck was I supposed to do?"

Aiden laughed.

"You're the one who always brags about my computer engineering skills. It seems they are looking for people like me."

"I'm siced," said Aiden, punching his fist into the palm of his hand. "How long is the waiting list?"

"I don't know, but at least I'm on it. Check this out." A holo-image of the grey-eyed girl Aiden had a crush on for two years appeared beside Coulter's face. He turned to it and pretended to kiss it passionately.

"Yuck. Do you really need to use your tongue with that?"

"That's for emphasis. I thought that would make your day. She moved. Now we don't have to share our love for her anymore. We can call off the duel."

Aiden shook his head.

"That's it? Shaking your head? Is that all you have for me? Disappointing. I expected a better response. No, wait. I know you, and I know that look. There's a new one on your radar, isn't there? One that made you forget about all the others. Who is she? Hold up."

Coulter's head lowered. His eyes darted back and forth. "Got it. Is this her?"

Danai's image appeared in front of him.

"How did you do that?"

"The Institute's new student database. You know my skills, and I know your type."

"I have a type? I don't have a type."

"Yes, you do, right here on the screen. I need details—later, though. I got a ticket to ride the Alphatron."

"Oh, the new high-speed module? That thing is fast."

"Speed I love, but if it drops like a rollercoaster, I will pass out."

Aiden laughed. "How did you get so lucky?"

"It's who you know and what you know. Later, bro."

"Hey, check in on my mom when you have time."

"On it. I'll invite her to go out with me."

"Stop it."

"I haven't had a date in a while."

"Stop it."

"I have a type too. Is she seeing anyone?"

Aiden narrowed his eyes and gave Coulter the most threatening expression he could muster without cracking a smile.

Coulter laughed, and the screen went black.

They'd been friends since sixth grade. It made Aiden's day to think Coulter would join him at the Institute.

Now in a jovial mood, Aiden left for the eatery and sat next to Quest. He connected with each of his new friends in different ways. Quest loved music, all types of music, and so did Aiden.

The Institute permitted Quest to bring his equipment with him, and Aiden praised him for his digital mixes. Music was just a hobby. Quest's area of study was physics, driven by his obsession with travel between parallel universes.

"I think she tries to be here on purpose when you're here," said Lax, sitting across from them.

"Who?" asked Oui, while he quickly sat on the opposite side of Aiden so he could sneak a look.

"Aiden's cuteness," Lax replied while blowing a kiss in her direction.

"She's not my anything," Aiden responded under his breath as he glanced over at her.

"Then why are you blushing?" asked Bale.

Aiden hadn't seen him join them. Bale was the voice of reason that balanced their group. Because of his military school background, he was the epitome of order, which Aiden respected. He didn't joke around much, but if you could get him to laugh, you felt like you conquered the most formidable opponent ever.

Aiden watched the entrance for Farmer.

"Busted," Oui exclaimed as he bit into a croissant dipped in chocolate on the ends. He tried to catch every sliver of chocolate as it crumbled. Although his name implied it, Oui wasn't French. He was sure to become one of the greatest computer engineers of his generation.

"What? What happened?" asked Aiden. "I didn't see."

"Your girl tried to look over here at you on the sly. She failed. It wasn't smooth at all."

Bale waved his fork at him. "Go over there. We'll take care of this for you." They each grabbed food from his plate before he could respond.

"Something is seriously wrong with you guys," Aiden exclaimed. However, he didn't move. There was nothing he would do in front of a room full of people. He didn't work that way.

"Lax, how long have you been here?" asked Oui.

"About six months longer than you."

Bale overstuffed his mouth and talked with it full. "Who are all these other kids?"

"I don't know. But that one smiling over here with the bangs is my girl, Brooks. If they're not in your classes, they fall under a different program. We all fall under neuroscience, minoring in the science of our choice unless they find your strengths lie in a different program. None of these kids would be here if there wasn't something special about them academic-wise. The Institute brings together the most scientific or technological minds of the future. The others may be in the physics or aeronautical program."

"I've seen a couple of them in physics lecture," said Quest.

Aiden looked around at those in the room. "Is it me, or do some of them look like grown men?"

CHAPTER 13

The next day, Aiden awoke with a jolt. A blaring alarm resounded throughout the dorm. He leaped from his bed and ran to his door in his pajama pants. It slid open, and he dashed into the hall, hating the feel of his bare feet on the cement floor. The other dorm doors opened and students peeked outside. "What's going on?"

His neighbor lifted his hands over his ears and shook his head. "Fire drill?"

"I don't know," Aiden responded as he stepped back inside and reached for a t-shirt. Just as he pulled it over his head, Dr. Laribe's face appeared on the display wall to the right of him.

"For the first four weeks of your classes, we require all new students to attend five a.m. drill. After the first month, it is no longer mandatory, but we hope you will see the benefit and continue. Three no-shows will result in your dismissal."

Wow, they are strict.

A student's name appeared at the bottom followed by a question. *Oh wow, this is live.*

Dr. Laribe quickly answered the question. "The reason we do this is because of how research has shown exercise affects the body. You think better—clearer, you have more energy, you sleep better—"

"And you won't gain the freshman fifteen," Aiden said aloud. His smile subsided as his eyes widened. *Oops.* He watched his name and statement appear at the bottom of the screen. He didn't realize it was so easy to add to the feed. *Mental note, keep your mouth shut.*

"Well said, Mr. Quinn. You have five minutes."

Aiden rushed to his sink and splashed water on his face, then searched for his sneakers. Teeth brushing would have to wait. *Another mental note, keep things in a designated place, and you won't have to search for them next time. Now I sound like my mother.*

He dashed out the door. "Hold the elevator," he yelled.

Quest stopped the door, and Aiden stepped inside with him and Tristan.

"Man, this sucks," said Quest as he rubbed his eyes. He still wore his pajama pants.

Tristan looked at the control panel. "We would get there a heck of a lot faster if someone pushed the button."

"Wow, I'm still asleep." Aiden laughed and pushed the L button to take them down to the lobby.

About thirty students gathered just outside the glass entrance doors to the lobby. They hurried out. Aiden looked over at Lax, who waved, and unlike everyone else, was wide awake and raring to go.

"Good, we're all here," said a voice from the front of the crowd.

"Look at the surprise on your faces. Yes, I'll be joining you," Dr. Laribe said while jogging in place. "Do you know why? Because nothing here is done without support. Remember that when you have an opportunity to help someone through a tough situation. Mr. Petropoulos, come on up here and lead us on our morning jog. I'll bring up the rear."

Lax walked up to Dr. Laribe, tapped his wristband, probably monitoring time and speed, and started off. His girlfriend, or Bang Girl as Aiden called her, followed close behind.

They ran five kilometers with Dr. Laribe at the rear pushing those forward who didn't think they could make it. The pace wasn't too fast. Aiden imagined they were trying to take it easy on them for their first run.

He searched through the group for Farmer. His disappointment rose as he realized that she wasn't in his group. Then between two white sweatshirts ahead of him, he noticed a hint of a blue glow. *Farmer's beads.* She ran near the front, and her group was breaking away. He picked up his speed. There wasn't much they could say to each other while running and with everyone around, but he wanted to be near her, sharing space with someone like him.

Just as he was almost alongside Farmer, Halland yelled out, bent forward, and grabbed his extended leg. Aiden slowed next to him. "Breathe. Breathe through it. Don't point your toe. Flex it in the opposite direction."

Dr. Laribe ran past him with the slower runners and gave him a thumbs up.

"Okay, it passed. Let's go. They're leaving us."

"This isn't a competition, Halland. Let's walk for a minute, and then we can try running again," Aiden instructed. "Unless you're some kind of cramp freak. You know those things have a chaser."

Halland shook his head. "No, I can wait."

A few minutes later, they quickened their steps to a light jog. To Aiden's surprise, Halland still had the energy of a five-year-old and ran with ease despite the cramp. The run ended back in front of the dorm. It was a rule that everyone wait for the last person and cheered them in. Halland held up his arms as if he had just won a marathon.

Dr. Laribe patted him on the back as they reached the walkway out front. "Great job, Aiden. We'll meet at the end of the week to see how things are going." They bumped fists and Dr. Laribe jogged off.

"Where are you headed?" Halland asked.

Dr. Laribe turned, jogging backward. "To the rec center. My workout isn't over." He lifted his hand and turned, continuing his trek up the hill.

"He's a beast," said Halland from Aiden's side.

"What do you say we get breakfast?" said Aiden.

"We're funky."

"So what? We deserve this. It's on me," Aiden joked as they turned to enter the building, seeing everyone else had the same idea. He put his arm around Halland's shoulder as they walked. "Now explain to me how they let a kid in here again?"

"I'm not a kid."

"What are you, like four-foot-eleven?"

CHAPTER 14

Aiden arrived at his third class of the day as early as possible so he could stand on the stairs and search over the blonde, brunette, braided, curly, ponytailed, natural, and cropped heads of hair for Farmer.

He spotted her as soon as she entered the building. The blue flash of her beads gave her away. He jumped off the stairs and rushed down the hall, followed her into a lab, and took the seat beside hers.

Lax entered with none other than Brooks hanging from his arm. They sat at the back of the room. *Those two are inseparable. I wonder what Dr. Laribe has to say about it.*

Lax motioned a fist bump in the air. Aiden bumped back, then made a V with his fingers and pointed them at Lax and Brooks. He then pointed a finger at his open mouth and faked vomiting.

Lax shook his head and mouthed, *"Snark."*

Aiden laughed. He had already told Lax it was unnatural how much he and Brooks hung out, especially when Lax had eyes for so many girls. *Then again, if I looked like him, maybe I would too.*

Aiden glanced over at Farmer every few seconds. *How do I start?* He faced her, but before he could form a word, the lights dimmed and a three-dimensional image of a human brain appeared over each table and slowly turned. The room fell silent. Aiden peeked behind him. Even Brooks had stopped whispering in Lax's ear.

Farmer placed the palm of her hands flat on the table and turned to look at him.

Aiden straightened his posture.

"Okay, this is weird, but are you following me?" she asked.

"And who are you again?"

"Aiden."

"Your name is Aiden too? Is Aiden a girl's name?" he yelled, looking horrified. "Did they name me a girl's name?"

Farmer giggled and held a finger up to her lips.

Aiden whispered. "No, really, I forgot your name. I'm not following you. This course is part of my curriculum."

"Oh?"

"It is."

"Are you pre-med?"

"No. Am I in the wrong lab?" His voice rose again. He stood as Farmer shook her head.

"Mr. Quinn, please take your seat," said the lab assistant. "We are about to get started," he added as he wheeled in a cart.

"Hmm . . . Seems he knows me. I guess I'm in the right place, after all. We both fall under neurosciences," he said while sitting. "What's your name again?"

She smirked. "You know my name."

"Yes, I do, Ms. Farmer."

The lab assistant pushed the cart to their table and placed a brownish-gray brain on top. Farmer wrinkled her nose.

"What you are smelling is the preservation solution used to reduce stress, deterioration, and microbial growth on the organ," said the lab assistant.

"Smells good. I should dab a little behind my ears," Aiden said.

Farmer moved it away from him. "Please don't."

The instructor spoke from the front of the room.

Aiden tilted his head. "I didn't hear him come in."

"Because you keep talking," Farmer replied.

"Study the three-dimensional image of the brain," the instructor stated. "As you dissect your sheep brain, every incision will also take place on your 3D human brain. This will allow you to see any differences and correlations between the two. Sheep brains are very similar to the human brain, which is why it is the brain of choice for this study.

"You are now receiving your dissection kit. Please make sure it contains a scalpel, probe, and scissors."

A shelf stretched out from the table with a white cloth on top.

Farmer lifted the cloth to make sure everything was there.

Aiden watched as her fingers delicately brushed across each instrument. As she lifted her hand, he noticed her bracelets again. "Tell me about your beads," he whispered.

Farmer shook her head and pointed in front of them.

She was right. He needed to pay attention to the terms appearing to the right of the 3D brain as if being written by an invisible hand on an invisible board.

Anterior

Posterior

Lateral

Medial

Dorsal

Ventral

"You will use these terms to specify the location of various brain structures. We will begin by examining the meninges." The word appeared in front of them with the definition.

MENINGES - THE PROTECTIVE COVERINGS OF THE BRAIN AND SPINAL CORD.

Farmer pushed the tray to the center of the table and turned it to the side, so they could both view the meninges of the sheep brain. The three-dimensional human brain also turned.

"Dear, you've made dinner. Sheep's brain, my favorite. You shouldn't have," Aiden gushed.

Farmer couldn't help but laugh.

For some reason, Aiden had no problem showing his humorous side to Farmer. He wanted to become her friend and build her trust so she would let him into her world. He wanted to be the person she turned to over everyone else if she had a problem. That was his goal. Eventually, she would fully and freely disclose what she'd been through as a Sleeper. He wanted—no, needed—to know everything about her.

CHAPTER 15

When the lab ended, Farmer hopped off her stool and hurried for the exit without a word, as if she'd had enough of Aiden and his antics for one day.

Aiden hurried to catch up to her and stepped outside, shielding his eyes from the sunshine. His pace slowed as he looked up. *What is going on? The sun is in the wrong place. It's one o'clock. Why is it over there?* He turned his back. *Maybe I'm facing the wrong direction. No, that's east. The sun rises in the east and sets in the west*—something he had used since he was a kid to help him understand direction, like righty-tighty, lefty-loosey for opening things.

He rubbed his eyes and turned around, looking up again. This time, the sun was where it should be. He stood there for a moment and looked around at the students and instructors crossing the campus. No one noticed anything. *That means it's me. I think I need more rest.*

He spotted Farmer and ran. "Hey, Farmer! Wait up."

She turned and waited for him.

"Hey, may I ask you a question?"

"I might regret this, but if you must."

"Why the Institute? Why neuroscience? What's your interest?"

"You really want to know that?"

"That's why I asked. Is it too personal?"

She shook her head. "No, I'm just surprised. Uh . . . you know the family that adopted me?"

"Uh-huh?"

"They have a son. The sweetest kid you could ever wish to meet. Mentally, he never developed past five years old. So although he's twenty and six-foot-two, I still call him a kid, my baby brother. He can't talk, but he understands and lets you know things in his own way."

"What happened to him?"

"He has ASD."

"ASD?"

"Autism Spectrum Disorder."

"Oh, Autism."

She nodded. "One morning there was something different about him. I can't explain it, but I noticed something was off. I witnessed him have a grand mal seizure. It was horrible."

"I'm sorry."

"An ambulance came for him, which made things worse because he has to be in the environment he's used to, or he gets upset. It was the first time I saw him cry." She looked away. "It broke my heart. There must be a way to help him and kids like him. I have to find a way."

Aiden marveled at the way she said it. There was no doubt she would accomplish what she set out to do. "You want to save him?"

"It's he that has saved me. He and his family. You have no idea what I've been through or the person I was before they adopted me. I want to help him communicate."

"Farmer, I didn't mean to upset you."

"It's okay," she said, rubbing her eyes. "It's not your fault. I've never told anyone any of this. It was good to actually talk about it, so thank you."

"You can talk to me about whatever you want, whenever you want. I'm here for you. I mean it." Aiden didn't touch her. He wanted to, but—

"Hey, Quest is looking for you!" Fitz yelled as he ran up to them. "That new superhero movie is out. We're getting everyone together for a group trip to the cinema."

"Which movie?"

"*The Dawn.*"

"Oh, I've been waiting for that one. That's supposed to be good. I heard the Panther is a love interest." He turned to Farmer. "You in?"

"I don't know. I don't really go to—"

"Hey, we're all friends. It'll be fun."

"Danai already said she's going," said Fitz.

"Okay. I guess I'll go," Farmer replied.

"Good. Where's the cinema?" Aiden asked.

"Only five stops north of here on the Teslaloop."

Aiden nodded. "That'll work."

Lax approached with Oui, Quest, and Bale. "You guys in?"

"Count us in!" Aiden responded.

Tristan and Halland waved them over.

"When are we going?" asked Halland.

"Can you even get in without an adult?" joked Lax.

Halland ignored him. "Let's go Thursday. Matinee and student discount," he said with a grin.

CHAPTER 16

A iden went to bed early that night. He wanted no more instances of his mind playing tricks on him—the sun moving, and weird lights he sometimes noticed in the sky late at night.

He spent a few minutes on a visual call with his mother rather than the usual hour. She understood he needed rest and asked about the courses being too hard, as though he had been studying too late into the evenings.

"Mom, I've never had to study anywhere near as hard as other people. You know that. My mind works differently. You know that too."

He watched her, noticing the difference in her complexion from being able to get more rest and not having to set her alarm twice a night to check on him.

"Have you had any episodes since you've been there?"

"Not one. I guess happiness is the cure for this disease."

"Oh, so you're happy now?"

"Mom."

"Now that you're away from me, you're happy?"

"Mom."

"Is that what you're saying?"

"No, Mom."

"Is that the thanks I—" The screen went black.

Her avatar appeared in front of him. He accepted the call and her image reappeared.

"Boy, did you just hang up on me?"

"No, *Madre*. We got disconnected," Aiden lied.

"Well, I'm glad you're doing well."

"Really?"

"Yes. What about the girl? Farmhouse."

"Farmer, Mom."

"Oh."

"I haven't been able to find out anything else yet."

"I haven't on my end either. I need the names of her birth parents."

"Detective Quinn is on the job."

"You know it. I need to know for sure she is who you say she is. Anywho, get to bed, mister. We'll chat tomorrow."

"Okay. Mom, you look good."

"Really?" She smirked. "That's what happens when people are happy."

"You're just going to switch it around on me. I see you. But, *you*? Happy?" Aiden shook his head. "Un-uh. You're miserable without me." He laughed. "Love you, Mom."

"You better."

That conversation was the last thing Aiden remembered before hearing the alarm again, blaring as if a bell wouldn't suffice in waking them. "It's too early for this," he mumbled as he put on his shoes.

I hope I have pants on, because I don't remember putting any on, he thought as he waited for the elevator. Oui and Tristan approached him. "Where's Quest?"

Oui shrugged. "I don't know. He was up late."

"Un-uh, somebody needs to go and get him. If we have to do this, he has to do this," said Aiden.

Tristan ran down the hall with Aiden while Oui held the elevator. "We have four minutes."

Aiden placed his hand on the panel next to Quest's door to announce himself, lifted his hand and placed it down again and again, announcing himself over and over.

The door slid open, and Quest charged out with his shoes in his hands. "Come on, what are you guys waiting for? And don't say you're waiting on me, because I'm already halfway to the elevator."

The usual crowd gathered in front of the building. Lax, Brooks, Danai, and Farmer were always there early.

Lax hit Brooks on the bottom as he ran past her. "Let's go, let's go."

I never would have guessed he was such a morning person, Aiden thought as he watched them. Brooks playfully swung at him and picked up speed.

Aiden wasn't in the last group of runners with Dr. Laribe, nor was he in the middle group with Halland this time.

He ran at the back of the first group, the elite, the gladiators. But when the run was almost over, and they rounded the bend heading back up the walkway, uphill toward the dormitory, Aiden thought he might pass out or throw up. Maybe at the same time, if that were possible. He slowed and leaned forward, breathing heavily, reaching for the ground. Suddenly, an arm grabbed him under his armpit, lifted him up, and helped him finish the course.

He looked up at Lax as he leaned against the brick wall of the building. "Thanks, man."

"I couldn't let you go out like that. I had to make sure you finished as strong as you started. Remember? Support? Like Dr. Laribe said?" He handed Aiden a couple of the water pods.

Aiden's lungs were on fire. He stuffed a water pod in his mouth and pressed it between his tongue and the roof of his mouth. The casing disintegrated as cool water released and soothed his scorched throat. He held the other pod over his head, where the heat and squeezing motion from his hand made it burst. "Ah," he whispered as the water ran down his face.

While everyone else cheered on those who were still running up the hill, Aiden brushed his wet hair out of his face and looked around the group for Farmer. He found her bent forward in front of Danai, stretching. *Look away, look away*, he told himself. But his eyes wouldn't listen to his brain. They traced from her shorts down the length of her leg. As he took a step toward her, a hand slapped him on the back.

"How about you join me at the gym today," said Dr. Laribe.

"Right now?"

"Definitely now," Dr. Laribe responded while looking over at Danai and Farmer. "Lax told me he's been training with you. Don't worry, I'll take it easy on ya." He jerked his head toward the gym. "Come on."

"Okay, but remember you said you would take it easy on me. And just so you know, I'm going to need as much food as possible immediately afterward."

Dr. Laribe laughed and handed him another water pod. "Don't shower with this one, drink it."

CHAPTER 17

Take it easy on him? Dr. Laribe didn't know the first thing about taking it easy on anyone. He put Aiden through a nonstop circuit of weight machines and kept increasing the weight. By the time they finished, Aiden didn't care about food or anything else. Danai could have passed by him naked. Instead of leering, he would have thrown a dumbbell at her.

All he wanted was to lie down. His arms and legs felt like loose rubber bands. However, Dr. Laribe showed no sign of fatigue.

"Good job, Aiden. The juice bar is open now. Let's get a protein smoothie before we head out."

I have a class in an hour, and you don't. I still need to lie down, and you want a smoothie? "Okay."

"Good, it will help with recovery."

Lactic acid.

"Yes, lactic acid. Did you just say that or was I thinking it aloud?" asked Dr. Laribe, confused. "Anyway, lactic acid is the cause of the burning you felt during the workout. During recovery, your body will clear the lactate and other metabolites . . ." Dr. Laribe looked at Aiden, and then up at the ceiling as if remembering something. "Of course, someone with a mind like yours already knew that."

Aiden nodded.

They went to the lobby and sat at a table next to the juice bar. Dr. Laribe ditched his straw and lid and gulped his drink. "Don't worry, you're young. You won't be as sore as someone my age would be. I doubt you'll even be sore at all."

Aiden sipped his smoothie and nodded. His eyelids felt weighted down as he listened to Dr. Laribe go on and on about his curriculum and then tell him about some earthquake he experienced. *Man, I don't care right now. How do I tell him I need to go?*

"Excuse me a minute." Dr. Laribe rose and greeted a student he recognized.

The campus was peaceful as the first light of day shone over the buildings. Aiden stared out the window as he continued to sip his drink, listening to the hum of the machines behind the juice bar.

Suddenly, he felt someone violently shaking him and calling his name. "Wh—What happened?"

Students were running out of the building, others looked panicked.

"I think we had a small earthquake. You dozed off," said Dr. Laribe. "I've been trying to wake you to get you out of here." He glanced at the ceiling. "It's over now, I think. You were really sleeping hard."

"I'm sorry," Aiden said as he stood and backed away.

"No, *I'm* sorry. I shouldn't have worked you so hard."

"I've got to get to class." Aiden turned and ran out the door. *Stupid! What did you do? Get some coffee. That can't happen again.*

CHAPTER 18

O verstimulated was putting it mildly after three sixteen-ounce cups of coffee. Aiden finished his last class of the day a little jittery, walking at a hurried pace through the quad, carrying on conversation with anyone who could understand fifty words in two seconds, and ready to take on every project his professors had assigned, in one night.

He passed by students talking about the biggest news of the day, the earthquake only he knew he'd caused. *From now on, no matter what, I have to get proper rest,* he thought as he entered the dorm lobby.

He glanced over at the lounge area and noticed a student with his head down, resting atop his folded arms on a table. *Tapered afro. Is that Quest? I guess I wasn't the only one worn out today*, he thought as he sat in the chair beside him.

"Quest!" Aiden shouted.

Quest didn't move.

Aiden shook him. "Quest!"

Still no movement.

Is he breathing? Aiden lowered his head next to Quest's. He snored softly. *I guess he's a hard sleeper. I need to brush up on friendship etiquette. Do I leave him here or stay with him?*

Aiden stayed. He sat back and looked through the windows at the courtyard. It was a great day to test out the hoverboards parked near the cycle racks. He'd ask Quest about joining him later.

A girl passed in front of him and smiled. Something about her reminded him of Farmer. He wondered where she was.

Before he could give it any more thought, shrieking came from outside. "What was that?" Aiden stood, looking around the lobby as students pointed toward the windows facing the courtyard.

Someone screamed, and everyone ran to check it out. Aiden couldn't believe his eyes. A seven-foot-tall creature stood a few feet from the building. Its skin was grey, and its small chin and slanted almond eyes were disproportionate to its large head. Its stance was threatening—legs apart, chest lifted with its right shoulder and arm turned away, possibly hiding a weapon on that side. It was an alien and not the friendly kind that wants to phone home or be allies and perhaps share the earth, but the scary kind. The kind that stands over your bed at night watching you, steals your children, and runs experiments on you that you don't remember.

In his head, a voice whispered, "Run." Then it exploded in his ear, "Run!" Aiden didn't listen. He couldn't tear his eyes away from the alien, who lifted its hand, releasing small objects, as if parting from its skin. They shot at the fountain in the middle of the square that a few kids hid behind. Everyone around Aiden screamed as the fountain exploded. The cloud of dust quickly dissipated, revealing the kids lying on the ground, wet and covered in fine particles.

Maybe the earthquake wasn't caused by me, but by this thing coming from underground or warping in or its spaceship landing or something.

The alien took a few steps toward Aiden's dorm. It watched the students at the windows, its body as still as a statue. Only its eyes turned.

That's creepy. It looks like it's not sure what it wants to do.

"This can't be happening," a guy next to Aiden whispered to himself.

"Truth is stranger than fiction . . . ."

The guy looked at Aiden as if he just realized someone was next to him.

"Mark Twain," Aiden said. "Look!"

Campus security approached from the opposite end of the courtyard. Shots were fired.

Aiden tapped on his wristband to snap a photo and looked back over the heads behind him at Quest. *He's missing everything. How is he sleeping through all of this?*

Aiden's jaw dropped. *Quest is sleeping through this.* His eyes widened as he turned away from the window and faced Quest.

He pushed his way through the crowd, ran to Quest, and searched his pockets for his remote CPU-bot. Quest always carried it. He found it in his back pocket. Aiden pressed Quest's finger against the screen to unlock the bot and searched for what Quest had watched the night before or even that day. It would be the first thing listed in the viewed section.

Got it.

There on the trailer photo was the same alien that stood outside, manipulating something.

What is happening? The feeling of pins and needles spread across Aiden's arms and legs. Everyone in the lobby yelled as they rose from the floor, floating in the air. Aiden grabbed onto Quest, who rose in the same position he was in at the table.

The screech of metal bending and tearing apart overpowered the screaming of the students. Glass shattered as the wall of windows separated from the ceiling. Aiden yelled out to Quest and tried to shake him, which was almost impossible while rising in the air.

"It's trying to take us!" someone yelled.

I've got to wake him up! Aiden reached over and slapped Quest as hard as he could as the alien charged toward the lobby.

Quest, wake the heck up!

Quest's eyes shot open, and the alien immediately disappeared. At the same time, all the floating students dropped to the ground.

Aiden rolled over onto his back, moaning.

"Wake the heck up," Quest groaned.

"What?"

"That's what I heard you say."

Aiden sat up. *I was thinking it, but did I say it?*

"What happened?" asked Quest, in agony from hitting the ground chest first.

"An alien invasion."

Aiden didn't let on that he knew what had happened. He stayed with Quest until he was checked out by the campus paramedics. Quest didn't want to talk, so after finding out he was okay, Aiden left him and went to his room for the rest of the evening.

News spread quickly all over campus that the whole alien thing had all been a hoax carried out by one of the campus clubs. *What hoax levitates people,* thought Aiden. *First Farmer and now Quest. The three of us, Sleepers. The only ones in the world.* He thought long and hard about revealing he was a Sleeper also.

I could say something like, 'I heard about people that dream stuff and it comes to life.' No. It's not time yet. They were just becoming friends. If Quest wanted Aiden to know, he would have told him. *Your secret's safe with me, buddy.*

CHAPTER 19

T he next day, Aiden awoke expecting to see the first rays of the sun rising and pouring through his window just enough to say, "It's time. Oatmeal time."

Under Lax's instruction, Aiden's meal plan, created to coordinate with his new fitness regimen, included oatmeal for breakfast. He was not a fan, but now, as his stomach growled, he looked forward to the bland bowl of oats.

He rose from his sleep chamber like a vampire leaving his coffin and laughed at the thought. He suddenly stopped laughing, wondering why the usual sunlight didn't fill his room. Only a glimmer of light peeked around a shadow. *Either I'm up too early, or I slept in too late.*

"Ouch!" he exclaimed as he stretched and arched his back. His body still ached from being dropped from mid-air the day before.

Why is this room so dark? Sheesh. Did I sleep half the day?

Aiden's mouth agape and eyes wide, he slowly ambled up to his floor-to-ceiling back window. Peeking through tree branches was an enormous poster of *The Dawn* movie on a building. He took a step back, almost tripping over nothing. "That building wasn't there yesterday."

He turned and ran out of his room. He made it down to the lobby, which the Institute repaired in one day after the alien invasion, and out the door. Around the back side of the dorm, past the cycle and hoverboard racks, he stood in front of the three-story Student Union building.

"Aren't you cold?" asked a guy who had just exited the front doors.

Aiden looked down at his shirtless torso and his bare feet. That's what shock did to you, it jarred your senses. His eyes ran across the front of the building at the posters of movies that were coming soon and now playing, dance troupes that would come, and concerts. He stopped a girl that was about to pass him by. "When did this get here?" he said, pointing at the building.

"The sign?"

"No, the building."

"You've never been to this part of campus before? It's new."

Okay, it's new, thought Aiden. *But they couldn't have erected it overnight.*

"I think about nine months old."

Aiden watched her, scratching his head as she walked away. *Maybe I'm having a psychotic episode. Look at me. I'm standing out here in my pajama pants, bare feet, and no shirt.*

He shook his head. *No. I know I'm not going crazy. This building was never here before.*

CHAPTER 20

LAX

Two weeks into classes, and exams had already begun. The professors wasted no time weeding out those whose grades might not be up to par. Nothing below ninety percent was acceptable. The students were told the early exam scores determined which courses their strengths lie in.

Lax's messenger beeped and flashed when he entered his dorm suite. "Audio," said Lax.

"Lax, this is Professor Houser. I'm calling to give you a heads up that there will be a pop quiz tomorrow. The student who receives the lowest score on the last test is always alerted about the next pop quiz to give him an edge. It's a chance to bring your average back up. Press continue when you are ready to view the film on Dubai. You should watch it several times to make sure you don't miss anything. I'm sure you will find it informative. Good luck."

"Sounds like you have studying to do," Brooks offered as she pulled out of his arms and turned to leave.

He reached for her. "No, don't go. I can get to that later."

"Not if I stay, you won't. I like smart men, remember? Study."

Lax grabbed her hand and pulled her back. She stumbled into his arms and looked up at him.

Brooks had attended the Institute a year longer than Lax. They'd had an instant connection after meeting in the weight room at the rec center. She introduced him to other students and showed him around. It wasn't long before they were dating. He called it his first grown-up relationship.

Lax moved her bangs away from her eyes. "Okay, whatever you say."

She kissed him on the jaw and pulled away. "I'll see you tomorrow."

He pulled her back toward him and gave her his best pouty face. "Don't go."

Brooks grinned. "That's cute."

"Is it? I tried."

She kissed him again. "Study," she said as she pulled away and jumped back out of his reach. "And you know I'm not the least bit ready for what you're trying to keep me here to do."

"Who me?" Lax asked, innocently.

She laughed. "Yes, you. Go on. Get to work. I'll see you tomorrow."

Lax watched the door slide closed behind her and then replayed Professor Houser's message. He sighed. *How is ninety a low score?*

The film was interesting enough for Lax to watch three times. A documentary on the history of digital technology in Dubai. There was information on a crime lord—detailing his ruthlessness, how his criminal endeavors had destroyed families and communities.

The film stressed that someone needed to stop him before more lives were lost. His name, Oracle Lurssen, continually flashed on the display, followed by his location. He vacationed at sea on the Eclipse Hotel Sea Resort in the Persian Gulf.

Lax appreciated the heads-up. Any opportunity to get his grades as high as possible and please his grandfather excited him. He studied so late that when he finally closed his eyes, he quickly drifted into a sound sleep. Within ninety minutes, he entered REM sleep status and dreamed...

He flew through the brightest blue sky he'd ever seen. The wind felt damp as it blew over his face. He soared through clouds and descended over Dubai, marveling at the second tallest building in the world, Burj Khalifa, as he flew around it. The sunlight reflecting off the windows caused the building to glisten.

He flew over the remains of the Palm Islands, away from the coast, and soared over the Persian Gulf before shooting through the sea like a missile. In the blink of an eye, he stood inside the Eclipse Hotel and entered Oracle Lurssen's suite.

Lurssen jumped back at the sight of him.

"How did you get in here? Who are you?" He asked while stretching his neck to look around Lax for his henchmen. There was no one there.

Lurssen wore a robe and held a cigar as he stood in front of windows that stretched up the back wall of the suite to the ceiling, revealing the dimly lit ocean.

"Many governments are trying to find you," Lax accused. "You won't get away with the horrible things you've done."

Lurssen looked Lax up and down, amused. "You're wearing a cape! Who do you think you are—some kind of vigilante?" He reached uner his robe behind his back, and then under a table. "This suite is not the same as it was a moment ago. What's happening here?"

"Were you looking for these?" Lax asked, holding up Lurssen's pistols.

Seawater ran down the walls around the room.

"Are we sinking?" Lurssen pushed a button on the wall to reach the concierge. "Move out of my way," he yelled as he tried to shove Lax to the side.

Lax didn't budge. He grabbed Lurssen and flung him toward the back windows. Lurssen hit the wall hard and slid to the floor.

Lax repeated what he'd heard on the documentary in the same voice the moderator had used. "You must pay for what you have done."

His arms bent, his palms open and facing each other, Lax closed his hands together in a hard clasp. The room folded in on itself and Lurssen.

Lax startled awake. He jumped and blinked hard. He thought he saw the face of a girl looking down at him, and that wasn't the first time. Perspiring as if he had just gone for a run, he wiped the sweat from his forehead, sat up, and chuckled to himself as he rubbed his hand over his face. "Whew, that was weird."

Lax spoke aloud. "Call Aiden Quinn."

After three beeps, he heard Aiden's voice. "Hey, Lax."

"What's wrong with your voice?"

"I don't know. What do you hear?"

"I don't know. You don't sound right. Come to my room."

"Now?"

"Yes, now. Hurry up." Lax disconnected the call.

Lax's door slid open before Aiden could place his hand on the module to announce himself. "I had the wildest night."

Aiden stared at Lax standing before him without a shirt. "Dude, you have the body of a Greek god."

"Ha! You're just saying that because I'm Greek." He shook his head as he put his arms through the sleeves of his T-shirt and pulled it down over his head.

"All I'm saying is, you need to cut back on the anabolic-roids." Aiden laughed. "Seriously, look at me and look at you." Aiden flexed his muscles.

Lax laughed and sat in a chair. "You'll start growing soon. We have to keep up with your program."

Aiden looked around. "Your room is just like mine, just the opposite configuration. Cool."

"All the rooms are exactly alike. I didn't call you over to talk about my physique or the rooms or feng shui or whatever else you may be thinking about."

Aiden rolled his eyes. "Well, what's up? What happened last night?" He leaned forward. "Did you have a girl in here? I mean other than Bang Girl?"

"You mean Brooks. She has a name." Lax remembered the girl's face he saw as he awoke. The redhead. "And no, but I had the craziest dream. It seemed so real. I found this guy, a criminal the government has been trying to track down, and killed him."

"Okay. You were a vigilante. What's the problem?"

"I don't know, it was just weird. It was—it was so real."

"How did you know about him? Did you watch a movie before bed?"

"He was in a documentary about Dubai, and I dreamed about it."

"See, that's why I'm careful about what I let into my head before bed."

Lax stood from the chair, and it receded into the wall. "Yeah, I probably should check out my chamber. I was sweating like a hog in there." He pushed on a panel and his chamber glided out of the wall.

Aiden looked at him in shock. "Chamber? As in sleep chamber? Are-are you a Sleeper?"

"Yeah," said Lax. "How do you know what a Sleeper is? I thought I would have to explain to you why I don't sleep on a normal bed and that this isn't some kind of spaceship."

"Lax, I'm a Sleeper, and so is Farmer and Qu—I mean Farmer and there may be another."

"You've got to be kidding. I've never met another Sleeper. I didn't know another one existed."

They stared at each other. "Is this a coincidence that we're here together?" asked Aiden.

"I don't know. Possibly."

"Wait, how did the criminal die?"

"Smashed in a sinking hotel."

Aiden looked around at the floor. "But there's no water residue here. What we dream comes to us. Maybe it was just a dream."

"You're right," said Lax, feeling relieved.

Aiden stared at the sleep chamber.

"Hey man, I can see your mind at work, but we've got to get to class. We don't need a late credit on our records," Lax said and strode to the door.

He was certain they were having similar thoughts as they left his room. *What are the odds that another Sleeper exists, in most of the same classes, or in the same school, for that matter?*

CHAPTER 21

"I am not the only Sleeper," Aiden found himself repeating throughout the day. "There are three others. I can't believe it." He smiled to himself. It was almost an exhilarating feeling, like finding out your favorite entertainer has invited you backstage, or like finding your long-lost siblings or parents.

Why did the researchers tell him he was the only one? More importantly, were there more?

He knew he could be impetuous, but he really wanted to meet with Lax and Farmer—Quest too, but Quest didn't know Aiden knew about him. Aiden dashed down the hall from his room just as the elevator door slid open. Danai stood inside looking confused, barely making eye contact.

"Looking for me?" he joked. *That was lame. Why can't I think of the perfect thing to say while I'm in the moment, instead of later when I'm alone and replaying the whole scene over in my head?*

"I-I selected the wrong option. I went up instead of down."

"It happens," Aiden replied. "If it wasn't for the lights, we wouldn't even know this thing was moving." He realized when he said it that sometimes it felt like the elevator might be turning. "So how are—do you—are you enjoying it here?" He blushed. *Sheesh. Why am I so nervous? I don't have this problem with Farmer.*

"It's better than I expected."

Aiden liked the little crackle in her voice. "Are you heading down to eat? If not, we could go for a walk…"

Danai hesitated for a moment. "Sure."

I'll find Farmer later. Stay in the moment. This kind of thing doesn't happen to you often—actually, it never happens to you.

They strolled along, paying very little attention to where they were going. Aiden pretended to admire the grounds, all the while looking at the huge Student Union building looming in the distance. *Maybe it was there all along.*

He glanced over at Danai. *I should say something.* "Are you from the DMV area?"

"No, I'm from Michigan."

"That's a long way. I heard it's freezing there."

"Well, it's not so bad when you're used to it. The summers can get just as warm as in the South, but autumn is my favorite. It's beautiful there in October."

"You're talking about the leaves changing."

"Yes."

"Are there still many trees there?" *Idiot. Trees? Is that all you can think of to discuss? Come on, be interesting. Be charming. Give her something to tell her friends about. You know she's going to tell everyone.*

"Up north is still mostly trees. Considering the whole climate issue, we've been lucky."

Aiden nodded and took a deep breath. "Would you like to have dinner with me? I know we won't be alone, but it would be nice to have you join me."

"I—uh...I guess that would be fine."

Uh oh, she hesitated again. "Okay, tell me all about the hideous guy you have at home and how he became so lucky." *Hey, that was good.*

"Had."

"Had? What happened?"

Danai looked down and frowned. Sadness covered her face as she kicked at a stone. "It's not something I want to talk about."

"Then don't," Aiden replied with a smile. "Let's head back."

Danai stopped walking. "Just like that? You're not going to press me?"

"Nope. Not at all. I'd rather see a smile on your face than that frown." *That's more like it, Casanova.*

She smiled at him.

"Look at that, your frown turned upside down again."

"Oh, shut up." She lightly brushed her palm across his arm.

Aiden tried not to blush. Any physical contact at all gave him chills.

"What about you?" she asked.

"What *about* me?"

"I want to hear your story." She looked away as though something embarrassed her. "Tell me about your girlfriend or lack thereof."

Aiden wasn't sure he cared for her choice of words. *Lack?* "I'm a pretty focused guy. A girl would have to be quite amazing for me to go as far as to ask her to be exclusive."

"Interesting. Amazing how?"

"I don't know."

"Beauty?"

"Maybe. Different. Special. The one."

"The one? Really?" Danai laughed. "Sometimes you sound so much older than the rest of us. You're a romantic."

"Well, would you rather be the one or someone's placeholder?" he asked with an eyebrow raised.

Danai studied him and then looked away. "I must be honest...I don't think I'm ready to—"

He held his hands up. "Hey, we're just friends getting to know each other as friends do. Is that all right?"

Danai looked relieved as she smiled and nodded.

You can do it. Just act like you've done it before. Stop thinking about it and do it. One. Two. Three.

Aiden held out his hand to her, and she took it. "Just a friend holding your hand," he said with a mischievous grin. He looked up at the sky. *God, please evaporate the sweat from my hand.*

They walked hand in hand back to the dormitory. The west entrance opened to a lounge area before continuing to the gaming center, the library, and the eatery. A man hurried to the left of them and through a door Aiden hadn't noticed before.

"Hey, what's down that way? Have you ever gone down there?"

Danai shook her head. "Maybe it's where the employees go."

"Maybe. Let's check it out."

They ignored the AUTHORIZED PERSONNEL ONLY sign that flashed above them, and entered a long white corridor with one door on either side just before the dead end. To the right was an entrance to another corridor. They stepped to that side and watched the man in the white coat as he approached the back wall of the hall. They peeked around the corner.

He needs to slow down, thought Aiden. *He's about to knock himself out.*

The white wall glowed with tiny specks of silver. "Do you see that?" Aiden whispered incredulously.

The man walked up to the sparkling wall and passed right through it. Blue light in the shape of his body fizzled and disappeared. Danai gasped and stared wide-eyed as the color drained from her face.

"Back. Go back," Aiden whispered while ushering her in the opposite direction. His heart raced.

The two of them looked like they'd just seen a ghost. "That guy just—" He stopped what he was saying as students entered the lobby, heading for the eatery. He and Danai stood in the center, watching them pass by.

Aiden pulled her to the side. "Tell no one. We'll talk about this later."

CHAPTER 22

A iden couldn't get his mind off what he and Danai had seen, the way the man's body fizzled through the wall and the blue energy it left behind before totally disappearing.

He and Danai sat in silence in the eatery. His mind too preoccupied, he barely touched his food.

Danai stood after completing half of her meal. "Uh, I'm going to go. I'll see you later?"

Aiden looked up at her. *How long had she been standing there?* "Yes," was his only reply, but his eyes said more. His eyes reminded her not to tell anyone, and she nodded in understanding.

Later that evening, Aiden approached Danai's suite and rested his fingertips on the identification panel. The door opened, and he quickly pushed past her into the room.

"Did you tell anyone?"

"No, and hello to you too. My day? How sweet of you to ask. It was okay, but weird. I saw someone walk through a wall. A friggin' wall! Can you imagine?"

Aiden shook his head. "I'm sorry. I just—"

Danai held up her hand and laughed. "No explanation necessary."

It was then he actually *saw* her and almost forgot what he was there for. He had never seen her look so casually beautiful. Her hair, normally in a braid with wisps of curls framing her face, cascaded over her shoulders. And he could see her skin. She wore a cropped white T-shirt with her midriff exposed. He looked away before his face flushed.

Danai walked over to her CPU-bot. "I've been doing some research. The wall is either made up of particles that solidify when prompted or just a cover."

"Cover?"

"Yes, like what you think you are seeing is not really what's there."

"So it's not a wall at all."

"Right."

"I don't—"

"Wait, look. What does this look like to you?" Danai tapped the wall to the right of her door.

"A wall."

"Yes, but when I place my hand on it..."

Aiden watched her and responded as she performed the action. "The panel opens, revealing shelves of processed foods and junk you purchased at the eatery. Why don't I have one of those?"

"You probably do, but like most men, you never thoroughly checked things out or bothered to read your suite welcome manual."

Aiden smiled while his eyes searched the shelves from top to bottom. "I'll have a candy bar," he said, reaching forward.

Danai slapped his hand away.

Aiden laughed. "I mean you have—what is that—eight of them?"

"Okay, okay. Go ahead. I'll be over to raid yours one day, when you find it."

"Ha! Funny." Aiden ripped away the wrapper as his eyes followed Danai back over to her CPU-bot.

"Okay, so that's the theory. Either it's a cover, meaning there's something else there, we're just not allowed to see it. Or if it solidifies, then it's an entrance to a place someone is trying to keep us out of. Either way, something is being hidden from us."

Aiden walked around the suite, churning the milk chocolate over in his mouth as he gave Danai's theory some thought.

Her suite was just like his but with more furniture and holographic flowers and plants. *A woman's touch.* He hadn't allowed his mother to add anything to his space other than the necessities. He'd told her he didn't need it, and if it felt too homey, he might not want to leave.

"Empty storage unit decor it is, then," she had said.

His head bobbed as he strolled to the beat of the music that softly played as he made his way toward the floor-to-ceiling window in the back of the room.

"That's a nice beat," he said as he stepped behind her Japanese screen.

"Wait, don't go back there!"

"Who is—" He stopped. His candy dropped to the floor.

"I don't understand. Why do you have this?" He backed up, not believing what he was seeing.

"Calm down. It's just where I sleep."

"No, you can't—"

"What's wrong?" asked Danai.

Aiden stared at the glass-covered capsule. "You're a Sleeper," he whispered, barely loud enough for her to hear.

He grabbed her hand and pulled her toward the door.

"What are you doing?" she asked.

"Take me to Farmer's room."

"Why?"

"I'll tell you when we get there." Aiden pulled her out into the hall. "Which door?"

She pointed. They walked four doors down on the opposite side of the hall. Danai placed her fingers on the identification panel.

Farmer opened the door, smiled at Danai, and then noticed Aiden. The surprise showed in her eyes.

Aiden almost didn't recognize her. There was color in her cheeks, and she wasn't hiding behind her clothes or hair. She'd pulled her sandy-brown hair up into a ponytail. She had been journaling, still holding a blue crystal covered diary, and a pen was poised between her fingers.

Old school, using pen and paper. I like that. "Come with us," Aiden insisted.

"Why? What's going on?"

"Just come, please."

Danai's head jerked toward him.

Aiden saw it from the corner of his eye. *What did I do? Did I not say please to her also?* "Come on."

They took the elevator up to the third floor and went to Bale's room, then Tristan's, Quest's, Fitz's, Oui's, and lastly Halland's. Aiden stared at the back of Halland's room. He turned back and faced the group. "We are all Sleepers."

No one moved, no one made a sound.

"We need to find out why we are here. This is not a coincidence," said Aiden as they all looked around at each other in astonishment.

CHAPTER 23

MRS. QUINN

"Coulter calling."

"Thank you, put him through."

"Coulter!"

"Ma'am?"

"See, that's what I like about you, *mijo*. No one says Ma'am anymore. *¿Cómo estás?*"

"*Estoy bien*. Your son is slacking though. I've been trying to keep us connected via visuals. Now I can't seem to get a hold of him. Have you heard from him?"

"I have the same argument with him."

"I tried to hack into his bot but—"

"Coulter, you know you're not supposed to do that."

"Yes, ma'am."

"Now that I've said what a parent and responsible adult is supposed to say, did it work? Were you able to get in?" If she was not mistaken, she heard a sigh of relief before Coulter replied.

"Not yet, it's the most high-tech system I've ever seen, almost like that of a government agency."

"Hmm . . . I'm not even going to ask how you know it's like a government system."

"Oh, you caught that."

"Yes. Look Coulter, I have a ton of work to do right now. How about I have Aiden get a hold of you?"

"Thanks, Mrs. Quinn. I know it's not the same with Aiden away. If you need someone to talk to or hang out with, I'll be your substitute son for the day. *Ciào.*"

That kid. He had almost brought tears to her eyes. *That was so sweet.* Coulter was one of the good ones. *There's still hope for this next generation.*

She sat at her office desk and pushed a button that would dial Aiden. It was Aiden's idea to give her a short call or message every night. At least every other night. After all, he was still a minor.

When she talked to him, he always seemed rushed and too busy for her. She liked that he was enjoying his studies and campus activities, and that he had new friends, but she missed him. And it was quite an adjustment for her to go from knowing absolutely everything about her child's life to hardly anything at all.

His informing her that there were other Sleepers was mind-boggling, and the fact that they were at the Institute with Aiden had left her uneasy. Just knowing what they could do alarmed her. She had to find out where they came from. There was a connection between them that the Institute may have known of—the reason he got accepted in the first place. She didn't want to lay all that on Aiden. Not yet, anyway. She owed it to him to have all the facts before she pulled him out of there.

She rubbed her forehead. *Maybe it's time to tell him the truth.*

CHAPTER 24

A fter a week of unsuccessful contact, Mrs. Quinn called the Institute to request a meeting with Dr. Laribe, who was unavailable. A virtual assistant pulled up Aiden's schedule and informed her that Aiden's lab would be undergoing a scientific experiment that day involving a sleep study.

Mrs. Quinn protested and stood pointing her finger at the wall as if there were a person in front of her. "You get my son on this call right now. He does not have my permission to undergo a sleep study. Have you even read his file?"

"Mr. Quinn is in a lecture. I suggest you review the forms you signed giving permission to take part in experiments."

"Administering the experiments, not being experimented on!"

"I suggest you discuss this further with Dr. Laribe."

"That is what I have been trying to do, but—"

"May I put you through to him?"

"Please." *Finally.*

"Dr. Laribe is not available to take your call. There are four time slots appearing in front of you. Please select one and Dr. Laribe will return your call at that time."

Four buttons floated in front of Mrs. Quinn. Red numbers outlined in a red square. The time slots were each a half hour apart. *He will need more than a half hour for what I have to say.*

She tapped at the first button, nine-forty-five. *UNAVAILABLE* flashed in yellow where the button had been. The same happened for each slot.

"We are very sorry, but Dr. Laribe is not available to take your call today. There are four time slots appearing in front of you. Please select one, and Dr. Laribe will return your call tomorrow at that time."

Mrs. Quinn disconnected the call in a fit of rage, grabbed her jacket, and ran out of her home, mumbling to herself all the way to the elevator. Once outside the building, she looked both ways, as if she couldn't determine which way to go.

I've got to get to him. What if he has an episode, was all she could think as she jogged to the nearest travelator and stepped on it, wishing it would move faster.

She looked over the side at the skywalk below. A river of cycles and two-wheelers passed below her. On that level, you would think you were in the Netherlands rather than D.C. bike country. *I could use one of those right now.*

She stepped off the travelator and picked up a jog, pushing past people, and headed for the nearest Teslaloop station.

Mrs. Quinn arrived at the Institute in the early afternoon. She ran up the stairs to the entrance and pulled on the brass handles of the huge mahogany doors. *Why are they locked in the middle of the day?* She continued to yank on the handles while her eyes frantically searched the stone walls for a doorbell or identification panel. Finding neither, she leaned her body against the door and stood on the tips of her toes, attempting to peer through the glass at the top of the doors.

Frustrated, she walked toward the fountain behind her. *Why is there no one around?* The grounds and even the air was still, as if abandoned.

A stone at the base of the fountain caught her eye. She picked it up and hurled it at the small horizontal glass pane at the top of the door. The spot where it made contact sparked as if an electric wire had hit it. The stone bounced off the glass like a ball and flew back at her. She ducked as it just missed her head.

Mrs. Quinn gasped. For a split second, the appearance of the exterior of the estate flashed to that of a silver, four-story, nondescript building that had to be a mile wide. Then it shifted back to the old stone and brick mansion.

She backed up and rubbed her eyes. *Huh?*

CHAPTER 25

"Class," announced Ms. Genova, "each student will take part in a neuro-logical scan today for a study. The procedure will put you to sleep for just a few minutes, and then you will awaken."

Aiden and the other Sleepers looked around at each other.

Halland shrugged. "It's just for a couple minutes. What harm could that do?"

Aiden nodded in agreement. "Excuse me, Ms. Genova?"

"Yes, Mr. Quinn?"

"What is the purpose of the scan?"

Ms. Genova pressed a button, and her notes stood out in front of her. "The experiment will show how your minds have conformed since you became students here. Your courses and living at the institute may not be an easy adjustment for you. It will show in the scan."

"Why can't you just ask us how we're doing?"

"Because your brain will tell us what you won't or can't."

Aiden looked over at Oui, who shrugged and nodded. Lax leaned toward him. "It's nothing, I've done a couple of these."

Farmer spoke up from the front of the room. "If the scans show, I don't know, an anomaly, what will that mean?"

Everyone paid close attention to how Ms. Genova would respond.

"It will mean we need to meet with Dr. Laribe and make changes to your curriculum and social activities, or you may withdraw from the Institute."

"Is it mandatory?" asked Aiden.

"I'm afraid so."

CHAPTER 26

MRS. QUINN

MRS. QUINN RAN ALONG the side of the administrative building, her feet pounding along the cobblestone drive. Just as she approached the corner, someone exited from a side door. She jumped back and peeked around at them.

Two men rushed toward the back of the property. The door they exited from closed before she could get to it, and there was no handle used to get in.

Don't want to let me in? Well, I'm patient. I'll just wait here for you to come out, she thought as she ducked behind the shrubs next to the door.

Ten minutes ticked by.

I couldn't have seen what I thought I saw. There must be an explanation.

Twenty minutes ticked by.

She looked down at the soil. *This is the cleanest looking dirt. Why aren't there any bugs out here? I should be running for my life from spiders and creepy crawlies.*

Two students left the building laughing and too engrossed in conversation to pay attention to anything around them. Like the men, they also walked toward the back of the property. Mrs. Quinn caught the steel door with her foot before it closed and grimaced from the pain. She looked back in the direction the students had walked, but they were gone—as if they had disappeared.

Once inside, Mrs. Quinn dusted dirt from her pants and smoothed her clothes and hair as best she could. She had to climb the fence to get on the property, and hiding in the shrubs left her stained and wrinkled.

She walked down the first-floor hall looking through the glass wall of each room for Aiden's class. *Why is every class empty?* She looked up and down the hall. *Shouldn't there be an administrative office on the first floor?*

Through a set of double doors, she found elevators and stepped inside the first one she approached. "Okay, down or up? Going down," she decided.

The elevator doors closed and then separated. *What was that? There's no way this elevator moved!*

She peeked her head out the door and back in. She saw no one in either direction. *Right or left. Right or left. Right!* She turned right out of the elevator and made her way to a room that resembled a lab. There were ten tables with ten students on them, electrodes attached to their heads, and they all looked to be unconscious or asleep. Mrs. Quinn burst in.

"You can't be here," Ms. Genova exclaimed.

"Yes, I can. That's my son," Mrs. Quinn said as she pointed across the room at Aiden. "Wake him up now!"

"It's not that easy. We're in the middle of a neurological scan."

"Oh, really?" She walked toward Aiden. "The same scan you could have given with him awake?"

A blue form of light energy lifted from the back of the table over the student's head, continuing down to their neck in an arc. A red ray pulsed back and forth through the arc over their faces. Images appeared over each student revealing their brain activity.

One student twitched repeatedly.

"Why is that happening?" asked Mrs. Quinn. "A scan shouldn't cause that."

Ms. Genova, looking confused, headed for the student's table.

No, this isn't right, thought Mrs. Quinn. She charged toward Aiden. Ms. Genova turned, seeing her and cut her off. Mrs. Quinn attempted to move past her when Ms. Genova grabbed her arm. "I can't allow you to interfere."

"Get your hands off me," Mrs. Quinn demanded. She threw her arm back and pushed the teacher with enough force that she fell into the table of one of the students and slid to the floor, immediately waking him and shutting down his scan.

Mrs. Quinn rushed to Aiden, put her hand through the blue light, and snatched the electrodes off his head before shaking him. He awoke easily, not the norm. *What did they give you?*

"Mom, what are you doing here?" Aiden asked groggily.

"Get up. We're leaving." She looked around at the equipment in the room. "Why are you running tests on these children?"

"Mrs. Quinn." Ms. Genova approached her with her hands outstretched in front of her. "Please, calm down. I assure you the students are fine. This is just a routine exam. It's completely harmless. I've had to have a scan as well. I would never do anything to hurt anyone, let alone my students."

"Can you not see there is something wrong with this picture? These are minors, and we parents have not turned over guardianship to this Institute. Therefore, you shouldn't do anything to them without parental consent."

"Yes, but if they were freshmen in college, which is what we consider them, they would still be minors and doing whatever they like."

Mrs. Quinn recognized Ms. Genova had a valid point. *Something's still not right here*, she thought as she helped Aiden into the hall. Security ran down from the other end.

"It's okay. It's okay," Aiden said. "Let me handle this."

"Let you handle it? Kid, if you don't hurry so we can get the heck out of here—"

"Mom, I can't leave."

"What do you mean you can't leave? Is that what someone told you? You know I will totally cut loose in here. Is someone—"

"No! Mom, please don't do that. Calm down."

"Aiden, do you know what those tests were for? It doesn't make sense that a 'school' is running tests on you or even scientific experiments, who knows. And is radiation involved with these scans? No, you're coming home."

Aiden grasped her shoulders. "No, Mom, I'm not."

She pulled him. "Aiden, I can't protect you here."

He looked at her quizzically. "It's not you that's going to protect me."

Mrs. Quinn stopped pulling and stared into his eyes but did not let go of his hand.

"It was only a matter of time before we would have to face this."

"Face what?"

"Someone finding out about me."

"Let's go, Aiden."

"*Escúchame*," said Aiden.

He continued in Spanish, "Remember the time I intruded in your life? I thought you needed to get married and I needed a father, so I dreamed of you with my favorite action hero. You found him in the kitchen making you breakfast, remember? What did you do? You poured ice water over me to wake me up and told me you were fine, and we would be fine, just the two of us, and that I had to trust you. I did, and everything was just as you said. We've been fine. Now *you* have to trust *me*."

Mrs. Quinn began to speak, but the words caught in her throat. She looked over his face. He stood a little taller than her now. Somewhere along the way he had morphed into a young man.

He's standing up for what he believes is right and what he thinks he must do. She was proud of him in a way. At the same time, her maternal instincts shifted her into protective mode and told her that right now he was still a child, still her baby.

Dr. Laribe approached them, jogging in front of a security team. "What's going on here? Is everything all right? Mrs. Quinn is that you?" His voice held concern as he looked back and forth from Aiden to his mother to the lab. "Ms. Genova, shut off that alert please."

"Yes, sir."

Mrs. Quinn pointed at the dean. "You know it's me. I thought I made myself clear at the orientation. Do you remember what I whispered to you? If anything happens to my son, I will become a terror that you cannot even begin to comprehend? I will burn this place to ashes?"

"Mom!"

She didn't take her focus off Dr. Laribe. "Do you remember that? Why can't I get a hold of you or any human being in this godforsaken place?"

Aiden spoke before Dr. Laribe could respond. "My mom was worried she hadn't heard from me and came for a visit. She sees I'm fine now. She overreacts sometimes."

He pulled her to him and hugged her. Before he let go, he whispered in her ear, "Trust me. *Te veré en mis sueños.*"

I will see you in my dreams? Mrs. Quinn stepped back, searching his eyes for understanding.

"Go," Aiden whispered.

She kissed him on the cheek and backed away, holding his hand until she had to let go.

It was his eyes—her eyes—that made her listen, made her trust him, not the situation or Dr. Laribe, but him.

"This is all a huge misunderstanding. I just sent my personal contact information to you so you can get a hold of me any time of day or night. I want you to feel at ease. Aiden is perfectly safe, as is every student here at the—"

"I want to know about those scans," she said, cutting him off while pointing toward the lab.

"Absolutely. I must attend to this right now. I have to find out what's going on, because this isn't my class. Otherwise, I won't have answers for you. I need to meet with all staff involved," he said with an open hand stretched toward the lab. "But as I said, use my personal line at any time." He turned toward the guards. "See that Mrs. Quinn doesn't get lost finding her way out."

"This way, Mrs. Quinn."

She watched what was happening in the lab, making sure the experiment was over before she left with the men.

Dr. Laribe looked down, shaking his head, and then up at Ms. Genova. "What the heck happened here? Is everyone okay?"

Ms. Genova nodded as the facility security director approached.

"I will take it from here, sir."

Dr. Laribe nodded and walked past Ms. Genova and into the lab, then began to remove the electrodes from the students and help them wake up.

"Ms. Genova, may I have a word with you in my office? Incident report," said the security director.

"Yes, of course." She turned back to the students, who were now awake and peering into the corridor. "You are dismissed."

Mrs. Quinn looked over her shoulder, eyeing Ms. Genova as she left. Security took her up to the main floor. As they proceeded past the classrooms, Mrs. Quinn glanced toward the rooms, and then did a double take. The hair on her arms stood on end.

There were now students in every room. Their heads turned in unison and watched her with blank expressions as she passed. When they visited the Institute, the orientation leaders had informed the parents that those in the hall could see in, but the students could not see out. She was not mistaken in what she was seeing. They were watching her.

Trude greeted her at the front door. "Thank you for your visit, Mrs. Quinn. I hope to see you again soon."

Mrs. Quinn stood outside the building as the doors shut behind her. *What am I doing? Why did I just leave my child in there?* She turned back to the doors and pulled on the handles. This time they opened. Trude stood in the same spot, facing her.

"Did you forget something, Mrs. Quinn?"

"No." She turned and slowly walked away, almost shaking as she fought against what was gnawing inside of her. She wanted to scream, fight, and drag her son out of there, but she didn't. She went against everything her instincts were telling her, and she always trusted her instincts.

It was because of what Aiden said. She raised him that way, to be compassionate and a leader. *Whatever is going on here, he knows something.* She tried to think like him, or what she would do if she were him, and he was just like her. *He will try to investigate. That could be dangerous.* If he had made the friends it seemed he'd made, then his reason for not leaving had something to do with them.

Aiden was supposed to be the only Sleeper in the world. Yet, there are other Sleepers here—together—at the same time. And they are running sleep experiments on them. Something is definitely wrong.

Mrs. Quinn picked up her pace, and then began to jog. The security gate opened as she approached, allowing her to exit. *They're watching me.* She looked around the gate and trees for cameras but found none.

The gate closed behind her, and she proceeded up the block to the stairs that led to the Teslaloop station.

She stood at the top, looking out over the grounds of the Institute of Anomalous Intelligence as a breeze gently blew along the side of her, signaling the arrival of the Teslaloop.

A tear dropped from her eye. *I should have gone with my gut. I didn't have a good feeling about this place, but he wanted it so badly. They're all a bunch of tricksters. Tests? I know all about tests. I know firsthand what they are capable of.*

She walked to the yellow line for those boarding the Teslaloop and waited for the capsule door to slide open. There were a few people that owed her favors. She had some investigations of her own to carry out.

CHAPTER 27

"Dude, your mom is a gangster!" Lax exclaimed as he turned to Aiden. "I wasn't under. I saw her take out Ms. Genova like a linebacker."

"Did she? Tell me that didn't happen."

"Ms. Genova was like, '*Oh*'," Lax said as he mimicked her falling onto Quest's table.

Aiden waited for what was coming next, ready to cut down and unfriend the first schmuck who had the nerve to crack a joke about his mother.

"Hands down, your mother is officially my hero. She threatened to eat Dr. Laribe alive," Quest said with a laugh.

"What now?" asked Tristan. They were all kind of groggy as they walked to the elevators.

Aiden was deep in thought. If he knew his mom, she would be up all night getting all the information she could on the Institute, its founders, and anyone attached to it.

"Now we eat," said Lax, slapping him on the back.

"It's always about food with you."

"Your point?"

CHAPTER 28

Three guards stood before the facility security director, a stout man with the stern look of a movie villain involved in a terrorist plot.

"Explain to me how a parent, or anyone for that matter, could get inside of a locked building, and then explain how she found her way down to the research lab. Where were your security teams? Is this the way we protect our students?"

"Cameras show she got in through the side door of sector five."

"There's no way in that door."

"She hid in the shrubs, waiting until someone exited."

"Waiting? For her to do all of that, what does she feel is going on here?"

"The kid said she was just worried about him because she hadn't heard from him."

"How did she get through the gate?"

"She climbed, sir."

"Charge it, and make sure there are eyes on it at all times. If anyone touches it from here on out, they will receive the shock of their lives." He rubbed his chin in thought as a voice announced Professor Houser had arrived.

"Allow entrance."

The office door slid back, and Professor Houser stormed in. "I would like an explanation. What happened in my lab?"

"Sir, I'm in the process of getting all the information on the incident right now."

"Were you able to get any readings before the scan was interrupted?"

The question came from a deep, distorted male voice on the holoscreen over the security director's desk—a voice you would expect to come from a dragon or demon.

"Yes, sir. All except for Petropoulos', but we didn't need his. He wasn't under yet. Take a look at the readout. Halland is strong, but Aiden is exceptional. He has the best neurological patterns we've ever seen," said Houser.

"Who is third?"

"The girl, Farmer."

"Mr. Quinn's girlfriend?"

"No, sir, he actually shows interest in the girl, Danai."

"I'm sure he does, she's pretty, but it is Farmer he truly cares for. Watch the footage of their interactions. You'll see he takes special care with her. We may need to use that to our advantage."

"I don't think—"

"Good, because I do not pay you to think about this. I pay you for your research. I've had enough of this teen drama episode," the voice stated. "We need to put them through exercises that will cause them to advance further. Then, we can find out exactly what they are capable of."

"What about Dr. Laribe?"

"What about him?"

"He wants answers."

"Then give him answers. Send in Ms. Genova," the voice barked.

Ms. Genova entered the security office and stood waiting for Professor Houser to nod or give any indication he knew she was there. She looked back and forth from him to the security director who was sitting off to the side in his own office. She turned away from his cold stare, noticing the thin streaks of graying hair at the top of Professor Houser's head. He didn't lift his head, speak, or offer her a seat.

She cleared her throat. "I must apologize for my actions, Professor. I was only trying to stop her from doing anything that would harm my students."

"You did well," he responded as he tapped his fingers on his tablet.

She tried to see what he was typing and jumped back when he looked up at her.

"I'm just completing the incident report," he said.

"But you weren't there."

"I have all the information I need."

"Professor, were those scans really necessary?"

Houser frowned. At first, it seemed he would let her have it, and she braced for the verbal assault. But his countenance softened, and he stood and motioned for her to have a seat.

"Ms. Genova, these are exceptional students. The government has taken notice of them and has asked for the scans. They have bright futures ahead of them and the government is already determining where they will be placed."

"The government is interested in children?" *I don't believe it.*

"You need not worry about that. I appreciate your work and the interest I've noticed you take in the students. The only thing you need to do as my aide is continue following my instruction. There aren't many teaching jobs left I hear, with all the bots and automated classes. You are lucky to have this position, and it pays well, doesn't it?"

She lowered her head. "Very well, Sir, yes."

With that, she felt it was time to leave. After all, he stood over her and said nothing more before taking a seat again.

Ms. Genova stood. "Is there anything else you need from me?" *And now he's about to look at me with that 'and why are you still here' expression.*

Professor Houser looked up.

And there it is.

"That will be all, Ms. Genova."

She turned to leave the office, stopped, and held up her index finger as she faced him again. "Perhaps we should see that someone in the department calls or emails the parents of new students to keep them better informed." She scratched behind her ear and squinted her eyes, trying to find the best words for her thoughts. "It would be a form of, uh, preventative maintenance, so to speak, so nothing like this happens again. That way, we keep the parents in the loop of things." She paused and diverted her eyes. "I think they would appreciate it . . . And it would make my job easier."

"Funny you should mention that. I think you would be perfect for the job."

"But a counselor—" She looked down at him, hoping her expression didn't say the *no* that her mouth wouldn't form. Her eyes drifted to his notebook pad and back to his face.

"No. Your idea, your assignment. I'll run it past Dr. Laribe."

Ms. Genova nodded and left the room, too confused to be upset he was adding more to her already full schedule. In the past, his physical stature, chiseled features, and green eyes had been enough to make her loopy, but this was different. *That couldn't have been what I saw. The figure on his tablet. It moved. Why would someone be listening in on our meeting?*

She looked back at the man who now stood in the doorway, facing the security director and Professor Houser. She slowed her pace and closed her eyes to help her focus. From the hall, it was nothing more than a whisper, but she heard it.

"What do you think?"

A deep, distorted, voice answered him. "Keep an eye on her."

CHAPTER 29

The eatery was packed, and students continued joining the crowded lines. The walls on the opposite ends of the room displayed food items and dispensed orders. Aiden had never seen it so busy—every available table filled with people eating, talking, and studying.

If the Sleepers were giving any more thought to what had happened in the lab, they didn't show it. *Good, because I'm done discussing it.* Aiden stared at his plate, and then at Tristan's neck as he swallowed his juice. With each gulp, a familiar pain began behind Aiden's eyes. *No. Not now. I don't want to do this here.* He inhaled deeply and exhaled slowly as he looked around the room. Certain students were always there whenever he and the other Sleepers were. Why was that?

Funky Girl, his nickname for her, with her afro, square face, and round glasses. Track Star, the Asian kid that was always heading to the rec center as if he had no classes. And Bee and Bop, the do-everything-for-media girls, two blondes that were always laughing, applying makeup, and taking photos. They and the rest of their crew were all there. And if Aiden wasn't mistaken, someone from each table or from one of the groups standing around glanced over at them from time to time.

He placed his fingers over his temple. He didn't want his friends to see him have one of his migraine episodes and didn't need everyone running around in a panic about it.

After a few seconds, the migraine backed down. *That's a first. A mini one this time. Or did I will it away?*

Danai walked over with her green tea smoothie and scone.

"Let me scoot over," said Bale, winking at Aiden and allowing room for Danai to sit between them.

Aiden felt warmth as her arm accidentally brushed and pressed against his as she sat. *She could've sat down without touching me. That was purposeful physical contact.*

Usually, he would determine it was time for phase three of his program, a system he put together after analyzing couples and their interactions at school.

Phase one meant talking to her to see if she responded to him. Then, *she* would initiate phase two. If it turned out she liked him, she would find any reason to be around him with random contact, meaning touching. Phase three would mean going on a date.

But things had changed, and his attraction to Danai was the least of his concern. Plus, she had already let him down easy. *She's only interested in friendship. So now I've been moved to brother status. Fine with me. I don't want to be a placeholder either.*

"Now that we are all here," said Bale, "tell us what happened today. Some of us were still under."

Lax told the story. There were eyes bulging, and voices talking back and forth at the same time. It was too much chatter and more talking than Aiden thought needed to be heard by those watching and listening in.

Farmer looked concerned and mouthed to him, "Are you okay?"

Aiden nodded once. At least *she* considered his feelings.

He tired of the incessant talk, especially the jokes about his mother. *I'm not even hungry.* He pushed his tray of untouched food away and rose from his seat.

"Hey, where are you going?" asked Bale.

Aiden walked away without responding and kept walking until he was outside. A few feet away from the building, he heard someone call out to him.

He turned to see Danai walking toward him.

"Are you all right?"

He shrugged.

"Where are you going?"

"For a walk," he said as he turned.

She ran to him. "I thought you might want to be alone, but Farmer thought I should check on you. How about I go with you?"

Aiden faced her. *Farmer thought? Whatever.* He realized he was frowning and didn't want her to think she was the cause. "Lax has a loud mouth. I don't think we should talk about anything in there. I think we're being watched."

"Watched by whom?"

"I don't know. Maybe by whoever is behind that wall. My mother is an attorney, and she taught me that in investigations, if you have a feeling that something is wrong, it probably is."

"I kind of feel it too, even before the wall thing." She looked back at the building. "Did you go back—to the wall, I mean? The one that man walked through."

"No, I did everything I could not to. They would expect us to because we are young and inquisitive. If we didn't report it or didn't go back and we were being watched, that would mean we probably didn't see anything."

Danai nodded and skipped to pick up her pace to keep up with him.

"Hey, your mom—"

Aiden put his hand up. "Let me stop you there." He'd had enough with the jokes.

"No, I was just going to say how much I can see she loves you."

He looked away, watching the tree leaves blowing. "The joy in my pain."

"That was deep. Not sure I understand though."

Why did I say that? He shook his head and waved his hand.

"No, come here. Don't disregard it. Tell me." She grabbed his hand and held onto it.

Aiden looked at his hand clasped in both of hers. He motioned around him with his free arm. "This life, the life we Sleepers endure, is full of pain. My mother gives me joy amid all that pain."

Danai smiled and let go of his hand. "That's beautiful. Thank you for sharing that." She shook her head. "You're right. We don't have an easy life. It's a life of guilt as well."

"It eventually ran my father off. I was too young to remember, but I guess it was too much for him. I've always blamed myself." Aiden watched her walk a few steps ahead as he spoke. There was always a sadness about Danai when they talked about home or the past. He noticed she added nothing about *her* mother or parents. "Hey, check this out."

Danai looked back at him.

"So, God—you know, the creator of all of this beauty around us . . ."

Their eyes met.

"Yeah, I know who God is."

"Okay, so he gave us to our parents so they could raise us—teach us and guide us in the right way. We were never really theirs but his, but he entrusts us to them—"

"Farmer told me you were a church boy."

"Farmer?" *They've been talking about me?* "Okay, anyway, so what if that isn't the case at all?"

Danai crossed her arms in front of her and raised one eyebrow.

Aiden laughed. "Wait, look. What if God gave us to our parents to protect us? They are our guardians because we, the Sleepers, are all the last of an alien race and they must protect us from the evil—"

"Hold it right there," Danai said, cutting him off before laughter exploded from her. "You had me. I mean, I was right there with you until you got to the alien part."

Aiden laughed. "I think I let the crazy out a little too soon."

"Yeah, you might want to hide it until you're married."

Aiden enjoyed watching her laugh, anyone really. It was one of those human traits he found special. He never wanted to imagine a life without laughter.

Danai's laughter subsided, and she became serious. "We need to tell someone."

"Tell who?"

"I don't know. Dr. Laribe, maybe."

"All they have to do is solidify the wall and say we were seeing things or on something."

"I just kind of feel like we should do something."

They walked along the park trail at the back of the property and sat on a bench next to the pond.

After a moment, Aiden cleared this throat. "We seriously need to focus on something else. I don't want to dream about this tonight."

"I agree."

"So, Ms. Michigan, if you could go anywhere in the world, where would you go? For me, it would be a beach. I would love to lie in the sand and swim in the ocean."

"And drink out of a coconut?"

"Or a pineapple."

"Oh, with the little pink umbrella in it and a surfboard under your arm."

"No more television for you." He laughed. "What about you? Where would you want to go?"

"Paris."

"Really?" Aiden wrinkled his nose.

"Yeah. What's wrong with that?"

"Well, it's uh—" He tried to find a nice way to say it.

"I'm talking about the Paris of old, before the terrorist attacks. Not the way it is now."

"Maybe one day it will be great again."

"Well, for your information, it *is* being rebuilt. It may take some time, but it will come back with all of its splendor." She stuck her tongue out at him, green from the concoction she drank at lunch.

Speaking of Paris made Aiden think of Oui. He jumped up, startling her. "Hey, I need to get back. I have to check something out."

CHAPTER 30

"I'm one step ahead of you, kid," Oui said while sitting in front of his CPU-bot. "I've made a list of all of us, our dates of birth, and where we lived at the time of birth."

"You could get to all of this information?"

"Of course. It wasn't hard."

"Any connection? Are we related? Cousins?" Lax asked jokingly.

Oui glanced at him with a straight face.

Lax snorted. "What? I know you're not mesmerized by my beauty."

Oui stopped typing. "You know that guy, the terrorist you told us about? Lurssen?"

"Yeah . . ."

"He really *is* dead. The report said he drowned."

"When?"

"The same night you dreamed it."

Lax fell back against the wall. "It *was* me. I told you," he said, turning toward Aiden with hurt eyes.

Fitz and Tristan rushed to his side. "It wasn't your fault. You had no idea. It's this disease," Tristan said as he slammed his foot on the wall behind him in anger.

They ignored the cracking sound that came from the wall.

"You're not alone, man. We are all in the same boat. But, for the first time, we have people like us that know what we are going through," said Fitz. "That makes each night a little easier to endure."

The rest of the guys nodded in agreement.

Aiden noticed a vintage comic book montage poster on Oui's wall. "We're the real mutants," he muttered.

"What did you say?"

"We're the real mutants." He pointed at the wall. "The comic book world is a lie. I've read enough of them to know. They should ban them. They trick you into thinking a world with superheroes—mutants—could actually exist. Like they could coincide with humans seamlessly.

"Now the villains, they're right on point with that. But a mutant would not go out revealing himself and saving people. No, he would hide out, isolate himself, and not reveal what he could do. When people found out about him in real life, they wouldn't thank him for saving the day. He would terrify them, and they'd call the police, who would send in the military, who would capture him and run experiments on him and probably kill him. That's the real life of a mutant.

"This ability is stupid anyway. Could you see me walking into a league of superheroes talking about, 'I'm a mutant?'

"'What's your ability?'

'I make things appear.'

'Cool, we could use you.'

'Great. The only thing is it only works when I'm asleep.'

'So you have to fall asleep and then whatever we need will appear.'

'Not quite. Whatever I'm dreaming about will appear.'

'Okay, so we have you dream what we need.'

'No, I have no control over what I dream.'

"I can see them now, speechless and staring until someone shoots a bolt of lightning at me and is like, 'What the heck good is that? You could dream about a bakery and a cupcake appears when what we need is C-4. You wake up and all we have is a cupcake.'

"'Not exactly. When I wake up, whatever I dream disappears.'

'Is this a joke? Is this a prank? Get him the heck out of here. What the heck kind of mutation is that?'"

"Aiden, calm the heck down and stop it with the mutant stuff," said Oui. "You're not a mutant. Everyone, calm down. Let's reel it all back in. We're all getting a little too worked up, like there's no hope for us or something. I'm sorry, but I'm not wired to think that way."

Aiden felt foolish. "You're right."

Fitz laughed. "That was funny though."

"It doesn't change anything," said Lax.

Aiden thought for a moment. "Whoa, wait. Lax, I don't think it's your fault."

"Why not? I did it."

"What if you were fed that information on purpose?"

The room fell silent. They looked at each other.

"Is that why we are all here?" asked Fitz.

Oui sighed. "I tried looking up Sleeper history. There were no Sleepers before us. Not even a mention of anything like us. The common thing about us is that one of our parents was administered a neurological drug that was being tested. We are the product of a genetic mutation that reacted to it. No one else even responded to the medication. One of Halland's parents was the last one to receive it. It's no longer being administered."

"How do you know that one of our parents was taking it? If it was secretly being tested, would they make the names public?" Aiden asked.

"Kid, I'm nothing if not thorough. I pulled medical records. Each of our parents visited a branch of a Neurological Treatment Facility in different places. I'm thinking the company behind the research expected some result in the patients, but it was the embryos that got affected."

They all looked away, hearing the cracking sound again. Everyone turned to Tristan. "What? I didn't do anything." The cracking made him turn to the wall. "It's coming form there," said Tristan. He and Lax backed away from it. The wall slid up, revealing a three-by-three-foot opening. The panel behind it popped out and slid to the side.

"What is that?" asked Lax.

"Is that an invite?" Fitz asked nervously.

"No, Tristan broke it," Oui said.

"No, I didn't."

Aiden spoke over him. "I don't think we're supposed to see this. That square is too perfect. This is someone's access into this room."

Aiden knelt and peered into the dark space. "There's a breeze blowing this way. Anybody got a light?"

Oui handed him a flash pin. Aiden shone it inside.

"What do you see?"

"A metal channel with no end in sight. I'm going in."

"Wait." Fitz grabbed his arm.

Aiden could see the concern on Fitz's face. "I'll be right back. If I don't return in ten minutes, seal the wall closed."

"No. You're not going alone," said Tristan. They all stepped forward to follow Aiden.

"Oui, it's your room. You stay here and cover for us. The four of us will check it out."

Fitz knelt, peered into the dark opening, and stepped back. Aiden was more inquisitive than nervous. He led the way, crawling through the tunnel that seemed like more of an air duct. Lax crawled inside, followed by Fitz. Tristan went in last.

As they crawled, every few feet they heard what sounded like a pebble pinging against metal.

"What is that?" asked Lax.

"Candy," Fitz responded. "I'm dropping them from my pocket to help us find our way back in case this thing becomes a maze."

Aiden stopped crawling. "It's splitting. Which way should we go?"

"Left. Go left," said Lax. They turned and continued through the tunnel.

"I'm going to run out of candies soon. There's only about one-hundred-ten of them in a bag, and I had already eaten some."

"Why do you know there's one-hundred-ten of them?" asked Lax.

"I was curious, I counted."

"We better hope there isn't a critter eating them as you drop them," said Tristan.

Fitz kicked his foot at him. "That would be you."

"There's a light ahead," Aiden whispered.

"What did he say?" Tristan asked.

"There's a light," repeated Lax.

The tunnel ended ahead of them. Aiden looked over the edge to find out the source of the light.

"What do you see?" asked Lax.

"It's like a pit. There's something down there."

"Whoa!" Aiden exclaimed as he felt something happening to the base beneath him.

Fitz's voice filled with panic. "What's he doing?"

Aiden and Lax yelled out as the panel beneath him gave way. He dropped into a pit. His arms flailed below him as Lax caught him by his feet before he could plunge to the bottom.

Aiden's heart raced as a strong blast of air cut off his air supply and lifted his torso.

"Back up," Lax yelled behind him as he pulled Aiden up and into the tunnel.

"Is he okay?" Fitz yelled.

Aiden lay on his stomach on the cold metal floor, gasping for air.

"He's fine," said Lax. "You good?"

"Yeah, thanks," he croaked as he lifted his head and stared ahead. "Did you see that?"

"What?" asked Tristan.

"What *is* that?" He backed up a little, almost kicking Lax in the head.

"Hey, watch it."

Aiden's eyes widened. In the distance, he could see something moving toward them from the drop. "Back," he yelled. "Back up!"

The boys scrambled in reverse as fast as they could.

"Faster," yelled Aiden.

Lax was the largest of them and had trouble moving as fast as his friends in such a tight space. Tristan backed up, feeling for Fitz's candy as he moved.

The tunnel split, and they backed to the left. Tristan's hands frantically searched the ground for candies but found none. "The other way! We're going the wrong way!" he yelled.

Aiden led the way now, crawling forward as fast as he could. They screamed as something slammed down next to them from the space they had just crawled from.

"Faster! Something's behind me," yelled Tristan.

They all screamed again and again as something slammed behind them every few feet. They began to cough and choke as the duct filled with the smell of sulfur. Aiden pulled his shirt over his nose. He could see the light from Oui's room ahead and lurched out of the passage.

Oui ran forward and helped him grab Lax under the arms and yank him out, and then Fitz, followed by Tristan. He slammed the panel back on the wall. The seal suctioned as the panel locked in place.

"My eyes burn a little," said Fitz.

"Stop rubbing them." Oui rushed him over to the sink to rinse his eyes. He wrinkled his nose. "You guys smell rotten. Was that a trash chute?"

"Tristan, what did you see?" asked Fitz.

"I don't know, man. I didn't have a light at my end. It was like the walls were coming after us and caving in." He looked down at his foot, torn sock, and missing shoe. "It got my shoe."

Everyone looked at his red big toe and burst with laughter.

Out of breath and leaning against the wall, Lax turned and looked over at Aiden, who was laying on the floor breathing heavily, sweating, and red from laughing. "What did you see?"

"A cloud, pulsing and heading for us. Like someone sent it after us."

CHAPTER 31

MRS. QUINN

Mrs. Quinn arrived at home, her right eye nervously twitching. *That's never happened before*, she thought as she touched the lid. She reached back and felt where her pants were split from climbing the Institute's fence. She was dirty and tired, but nothing would stop her from beginning her investigation that night.

After a quick hot shower and coffee, she was ready to get started. She pushed a button that would dial someone who could discreetly acquire private information.

"Hey, Jaxxon. Were you able to get anything for me?"

"Affirmative. Check your file. You know the one." He spoke quickly and matter-of-factly.

"You've come through for me again. Thanks. I owe you."

"You always do."

The call disconnected.

Mrs. Quinn used her iris scan to open the encrypted file. Before she could examine its contents, she received an alert.

Ms. Genova is here to see you.

"Thank you, Tab," Mrs. Quinn responded to the home assistant bot. She blackened the screen and clicked a button that brought up an image of her visitor. "Full search," she instructed her system before going to the front door. It slid open.

"And why are you at my door?"

Ms. Genova opened her jacket and placed her hands on her hips. "I would like us to get past what happened today. That was not the type of interaction I'm accustomed to having with parents. I was hoping we could make amends. I've come with some things of Aiden's. Maybe you have items you would like me to take back for him?"

As Mrs. Quinn listened to her, her eyes traveled from Ms. Genova's face to her abdomen. Writing, in black ink, covered her white blouse:

Not much time. I am being followed.

Mrs. Quinn looked into Ms. Genova's eyes. They were pleading with her. She held out her hand and nodded. Ms. Genova let out a heavy sigh as Mrs. Quinn stepped aside, allowing her inside the house. She peered into the hallway. She didn't see anyone, but that meant nothing. It was better to assume they were being watched.

The door slid shut behind them.

"The technology to see and hear inside walls doesn't apply here. You may speak freely. However, if you are being followed, their inability to know what's going on in here may cause concern. Let's make this quick."

Ms. Genova nodded. Her face looked drawn and tired. "Why do you have that form of security?"

"That's none of your concern. What *is* of concern is why you are really here. Am I the only parent you visited? It looks suspicious."

"No, I took and retrieved items from the homes of all of the students living in a close enough radius. I've been assigned to contact the parents, so this does not look out of the ordinary. It looks like I'm trying to get on top of things."

"To you, maybe." Mrs. Quinn stepped in front of Ms. Genova, stopping her from walking any further. "Nice jacket." She placed her hand on the lapel and gently ran her fingers down the edges and then inside the opening.

"Still don't trust me? In this day and time, if I were *wired,* as they used to say, it would be through a lens covering my pupil or an implant."

Mrs. Quinn stepped back. "My system scanned for those things when you crossed over my threshold, so I thought I would double check you for more primitive devices."

"Wow. How do you have that technology?"

"Again, none of your concern."

Ms. Genova shook her head. "I stopped at a department store on the way here. Everything I'm wearing is brand new."

"You suspected it also."

"I didn't want to take any chances—not after today."

"Did you talk to the other parents about this?"

"No, I don't even know what *this* is. It would be crazy to talk to anyone about it without knowing what's going on."

"Good. The less they know, the safer they'll be, I think. We can go to Aiden's room and grab some items. Follow me." Mrs. Quinn passed by Aiden's room and led Ms. Genova to her office. "I really hope I can trust you."

Ms. Genova nodded. "You can."

As they walked, Ms. Genova explained that that afternoon, she'd seen something she could not explain. "I'm not even sure I actually saw it."

After her meeting with the security director, she had gone to the back of the building and looked out the window. What she should have seen behind her was the next building. Instead, for a split second, she saw a railing and looked over it five stories down to active floors of people in lab coats. In the blink of an eye, it was gone.

Mrs. Quinn listened, but did not offer information on what she'd seen after she threw the stone at the building. Instead she replied, "Do you think my son is in danger?"

"I can't say for sure. All I know is that something is going on there. People have disappeared, including Dr. Tussaud—"

"Yes, I met him at the orientation."

"He's gone, and no one has any information on what happened to him or where he is."

"Did he quit? Leave of absence maybe?"

Ms. Genova shrugged.

In her office, Mrs. Quinn leaned over her desk and used the iris scan to re-open Jaxxon's file. His report expanded over the display wall. They both read:

There is no real history regarding the Institute, most of the information is fabricated. No information on who funded it. The property used to be a naval training facility.

Mrs. Quinn swiped her hand to the left, scrolling through articles.

"Where did you get all of this?" Ms. Genova asked.

"A friend."

"Wait," said Ms. Genova.

Mrs. Quinn stopped scrolling and backed the articles slowly in the opposite direction.

"There, stop," said Ms. Genova.

Mrs. Quinn stretched her hands, expanding a photo of a dark-haired teen with a muscular build.

"That's one of my students, Lax Petropoulos."

Lax's photo was in an old net article by an underground news source. Mrs. Quinn read aloud. "The U. S. Government is running scientific experiments on kids. Our sources say they call him a Sleeper . . ."

"Sleeper? What does that mean?" Ms. Genova asked, perplexed.

Mrs. Quinn didn't offer an explanation. "Look where he is—the lab. Does that look familiar?" Mrs. Quinn spread her fingers apart to widen the image. "Look at it. Is that the same building?"

Ms. Genova studied the image. "The equipment behind him. I've seen that in one of our labs."

"So what is it? A naval training facility or a scientific research facility?"

"I think it's both," said Ms. Genova.

Mrs. Quinn stared at her, and then ran out of the room. Ms. Genova ran after her to Aiden's room.

Looking around for items to give to Ms. Genova, she noticed his fish tank. *I keep forgetting to feed those doggone fish.*

She opened the bag Ms. Genova brought with her. "Nothing in here belongs to Aiden. These are women's clothes."

"I know."

Mrs. Quinn rifled through them and pulled out a white shirt. "Here, switch shirts. Don't worry, that one will go in the fireplace." She stuffed some of Aiden's things into the bag, including the *Moby Dick* novel she'd previously told him he couldn't read.

She glanced at the holographic clock on the wall. "We've taken too long. I have a pie that could help with the reason for the delay. It was too hot to transport or something like that. It's his favorite. Make sure he gets it, and, uh, you have a slice also."

The lines on Ms. Genova's forehead softened. "What will you do with the information?"

"I don't know yet. Watch my son. Watch all of them."

"I will."

"Don't try to contact me. I will get to you somehow. Take care of yourself," Mrs. Quinn said and hugged Ms. Genova before the door slid open for the woman to leave.

CHAPTER 32

"Where did you take her?" asked Lax.

"Who?" Aiden replied.

"Don't act like you don't know who I'm talking about. Danai. Who else? And don't try to deny it. I saw her kicking around with Farmer. She said something about a date. So where did you take her? Did you guys leave campus? You took the SkyTran to the mall, didn't you? Did you spend money on her? Is she your girl now?" He grabbed Aiden's arm. "Did you guys—"

"No, we did not."

Lax held a napkin to his eye, pretended to cry, and spoke in a flat, high-pitched voice. "My baby has become a man."

"You know that is not my mom."

"You're right. She's more like, 'I'll cut the tramp at the jugular.'" He laughed until he fell out of his seat.

Aiden laughed harder from seeing Lax get such a kick out of himself than from his joke.

Lax composed himself, breathing heavily as if he had never laughed so hard. "Really, where did you go? Did she let you kiss her? You went to the cinema, didn't you? Lame. Why does everybody always go the cinema on a first date? Hey, we can double."

"You really need to learn to stop after the first question and allow a person to answer. But no about the cinema. I took her to Paris."

"Paris? That war-torn, overpopulated, polluted place? How did you do that? A documentary?"

"No, back in two-thousand."

"As in the year two-thousand? How? Time travel?" Lax laughed and then stopped abruptly. "Are you telling me you took her in your dream?"

"Yeah, she said that if there was any place she would like to see, it would be the Paris of old."

"And you did what in Paris?" Lax asked in a way that expressed he was not totally convinced he was hearing correctly.

"We sat on the lawn in front of the Eiffel Tower and mostly people-watched. There were a lot of people picnicking. Then we walked along the Seine River and went to the Louvre." He laughed. "A street vendor took our photo, and then chased us with it, trying to get us to purchase it."

Lax stared at him.

Aiden stopped laughing. "What?"

"You really have no idea?" Lax shook his head. "I can't believe—do you know what this means? You can control it."

"Control what?" Aiden's eyes met Lax's. "I did, didn't I?" Aiden looked shocked. Why hadn't he realized it? And it wasn't the first time. He did the same thing the night before to contact his mother. That's why he told her he would see her in his dreams. He never doubted he could do it.

"None of us have the ability to determine what we are going to dream about and with whom, but you did," Lax said while poking Aiden on the shoulder. He jumped up, excited, and hit the wall. "This is major. Instead of a movie, story, or your emotions dictating the dream, you decided what to dream on purpose. And she was there and remembers it just like you? You shared the same dream! We should meet tonight. You have to tell everyone what you did and teach us."

"On one condition."

"What?"

"Do not tell Brooks about this."

"What? You're crazy. She and I talk about everything."

"Yeah, I know, but this is Sleeper information only. You will be breaking Sleeper code. No outsiders. Deal?" Aiden held out his fist.

Lax bumped it. "Deal. You think I didn't notice you called her by her name instead of Bang Girl. She's growing on you."

"Yeah, like mold."

Aiden didn't have to look at Lax to know it was time to run. He jumped up and angled his body away from Lax, just missing the swing of his friend's arm, and dashed out the door. Lax charged after him in pursuit.

"You better run!"

CHAPTER 33

The Sleepers gathered at the airball field behind the Zuckerberg Recreational Center. Lax had signed them up earlier in the day, so they were sure to get a timeslot.

"We've got one hour, guys. Set up teams."

The Sleepers formed two groups, five against five.

"That's not gonna work. Two girls can't be on the same team. We have to even it out," Fitz said.

Danai and Farmer looked at each other and frowned.

"Halland counts as a girl too," Tristan joked, pushing him into Bale.

Halland caught his balance and pushed him back, but Tristan didn't budge, as if he didn't feel a thing.

"Okay, Lax, Danai, Quest, Halland, and Oui on one team. Aiden, Farmer, Tristan, Fitz and me on the other," said Bale.

Lax adjusted the straps on his boots. "Sounds like a plan."

They huddled together as if they were discussing the rules of the game. Aiden told them what he and Danai saw with the guy disappearing through the wall.

"Whoa!" said Quest.

Fitz looked at Danai. "Nooooooo, that didn't happen."

"Yes, it did." She responded. "I'm glad there were two of us there to see it."

"Wait, say that again. He walked through a wall?" exclaimed Halland with his hands on the sides of his head.

"Unreal," said Bale. He stared into Aiden's eyes as if he could see inside of him and determine if he was lying or not.

With the assistance of Fitz, Oui shared what had happened with the panel of his wall and about the duct. Then Lax filled in those who didn't know everything that took place about the terrorist and the call he received from Professor Houser.

"So all of this, us being accepted into this special program, this place—it's all a sham?" It was more a statement than a question from Halland.

"Partially," said Aiden. "The Institute is real, but there's more to it where we're concerned."

"What are we going to do?"

"We can't tell our parents. We can't talk to anyone about this," said Quest.

"Why not?" asked Halland.

"That puts them in danger, if we're in danger. We don't know what we're dealing with."

"Yeah, all that we know right now is that they used Lax as an assassin. Maybe that's what they want of all of us," said Tristan.

The Sleepers looked around at each other.

"This is bad. This is really bad," Halland mumbled.

"I won't kill for them," said Farmer, her voice soft but stern. They knew she meant it.

Aiden looked behind them. "Start the game. We have a few onlookers." He motioned to Lax. "Did you invite Brooks?"

Lax looked over at the sideline, surprised to see her. "I promise you, I did not."

Brooks waved. He waved back.

Aiden stared at him.

"Dude." Lax crossed a fist over his chest. "Sleeper code. I stand by that. I didn't tell her anything."

"We have a Sleeper code now?" asked Tristan.

"Yes. Sleeper information is only shared with Sleepers. No outsiders," Lax replied.

"We needed a code for that? All righty then."

"Let's play," said Aiden.

"I'm not so good at this," Farmer admitted. Her boots glowed as she wobbled into the air. "This may not be a good idea."

Aiden grabbed her arm. "Steady yourself. Now, relax your knees. You're too tense. You'll rock back, and then you'll be flying upside down."

"Really?" she asked, frightened.

"I'm joking. Just stay still. Don't try to move forward. See Danai over there? She's not moving either. When the ball comes near, you attack. That means hit the ball at your team member. Otherwise, stay put. We will run it. Got it?"

"I think so," she said as she wobbled slightly. Her helmet shifted off to the side, half-covering her face.

Aiden adjusted the strap on her helmet, gave her a thumbs up, and moved forward to set up in formation. The opposing team's boots lit up in neon orange, and theirs in blue. "Your color," Aiden smiled while pointing down at her shoes.

Farmer smiled back with her arms out to the sides, trying to keep her balance before she toppled over.

Lax clapped his hands together. "Let's go, ladies. Let's get this game started." He turned to Danai. "No offense."

She smirked. "None taken, girlfriend."

Lax's hand slammed into the ball, sending it flying at Aiden's team.

Aiden glided forward and caught the ball. He looked across the field to see Lax making a beeline toward him.

"Open," his teammates yelled. Aiden ignored them and tipped the ball to Farmer. *There's no way he'll tackle her.*

Farmer floated in place, holding the ball and looking as if she didn't know what to do.

Lax's team ran toward her as Aiden's team tried to block them.

Aiden looked back at Farmer, who was still holding the ball. His eyes widened. Lax charged at her.

"Attack it," Aiden yelled. He and Bale were open for a pass. Lax was almost upon her. *No*, Aiden yelled in his head. *He's going to ram her.*

Lax's team began yelling for her to pass the ball. Aiden clicked his heels and shot full-powered across the field to get to her, but he wasn't close enough.

Farmer looked terrified.

As Lax reached her, Farmer dipped to the left, evasively skirting past him. Then she lurched ten feet into the air, flipped over both teams, and landed on the other side of the goal.

Everyone floated in place, speechless. Danai screamed and pumped her fists in the air. Oui grabbed her arm. "You're cheering for the wrong team."

"I'm cheering for girl power!"

"Noooo, did you see what she did?" Halland shrieked. "You've got major handles, girl!"

Farmer glided over to them. "Did I fail to mention I'm on the varsity team back home?"

Aiden laughed. *That was so cool. She's full of surprises.*

"New teams," yelled Lax.

CHAPTER 34

99 This would be a good time to huddle up again," Aiden said, noticing that Brooks and her spectator companions were gone.

"Halland had asked what we're going to do. That's why we're here tonight," said Lax. "As Sleepers, what we dream takes place in the real world." He pointed at Aiden. "But he is on a whole other Sleeper level."

Everyone looked at Aiden. "What? How? What did he do?" they asked.

"He can control his dreams. He's able to decide what he is going to dream about and have full knowledge of it while he's dreaming. He and Danai also shared the same dream."

Danai blushed as the others looked back and forth between them.

They became excited. "If we can learn that, we can come together as a team and defeat—who are we trying to defeat again?" asked Halland.

"That's what we have to find out," said Tristan. "Maybe this ability can help us. These people brought us all here, brought us together—which was a mistake on their part. We are all extremely intelligent. That alone would have been enough for us to stand out, but something else made them look for us.

"At first, I thought they knew about one of us, namely Lax, since he was here the longest, and did their research to deduce there might be others. But, from Oui's info, it's like we were engineered. Soon they will reveal who they really are, and we have to be ready. How do we do it, Aiden?"

"Wow, Tristan. Where did all that come from? You're like Sergeant Tristan," Aiden responded.

"In the short time that you've known me, have I ever seemed scared? Except, maybe when whatever it was slammed behind me in that tunnel."

Everyone shook their heads.

"I have never feared anything except being a Sleeper." Tristan's head dropped. "That's why—I know you've all seen my scars." He held up his arms, revealing his wrists. "I didn't want to live anymore. These scars remind me every day of what I am. But you know what? Once I found out you guys were Sleepers also, the world somehow seemed smaller and I didn't feel so alone anymore."

Everyone nodded. They all knew his pain and felt the new sense of being from knowing other Sleepers.

Lax ran his hand through his hair. "If they have us here because we're all Sleepers, what do you think are the chances they are going to let us walk out of here? Has anyone even left the campus since they arrived?"

"No," they each replied.

This is as good a time as any to bring this up, thought Aiden. "Did anyone else notice that as soon as we decided to leave campus to go to the cinema, a student center with a theatre appeared a day or two later?" He looked at his friends and swallowed hard, waiting to hear them laugh or tell him he was wrong or crazy.

Bale spoke first. "No one else mentioned it, so I assumed it was already there. But then I was like, how could I have missed a whole building of that size?"

"Yo, I walked up to the building, and I was like what the—" said Quest.

Aiden felt a load lift from his shoulders. "Why didn't anyone say anything? I thought I was going crazy. I couldn't even enjoy the movie."

"I don't know about that. That movie was good," said Tristan while fist bumping Oui. "But I guess we all noticed, the only ones on the whole campus who did."

"Actually, it's good that we didn't discuss it. They think we didn't notice. It proves that they're not going to let us just walk out of here. That's why it's important that we can control this ability we have." Lax pointed at Aiden. "This is the first step. How'd you do it, man?"

Aiden didn't like that they looked to him like some kind of savior. The last thing he wanted to do was get their hopes up that controlling their dreams was something they all were capable of doing.

"Okay, I've given some thought into how this could work," he replied. "We may have to make several attempts, but this is what we will try first. We will choose an agenda for the night and think on it all day long. When we go to sleep, it only takes one of us to dream of bringing the others in. We'll take turns. I'll go first, tonight." He glanced at Farmer. "Our victor, Farmer, can go tomorrow. We'll choose someone else for the next day."

"Wait, we're all future scientists, right?" asked Quest.

"What's your point?" asked Lax.

"We need to approach these experiments that way."

"Yes, exactly," exclaimed Aiden while high-fisting Quest. "Scientific method. Here's your chance to utilize what you've learned in your labs. What question are we asking here?"

The Sleepers began offering suggestions. "Can we all do what you did?" came from Bale.

"What are our limits?" Danai asked.

"What are we capable of?" added Lax.

Aiden nodded at each of them. "We're getting there, but what's the ultimate question?"

Farmer stepped forward and spoke over them. "Can we control our dreams?"

Aiden pointed at her. "That's it."

Everyone nodded in agreement.

"And," added Halland, "if we are capable of controlling our dreams, are we essentially controlling reality?"

The Sleepers were silent, thinking about what Halland had said.

"Who put a man-scientist in this little kid?" joked Lax.

Everyone laughed.

"Alright, Sleepers," said Aiden. "Tonight, let's all think about being together, and I'll try to bring you in. Remember—focus, concentrate. Let's hope this works.

"Do you guys want to finish the game?"

"Of course. We can't allow her to score on us like that and walk away," said Lax.

Aiden tossed the ball toward Farmer. "Your ball."

CHAPTER 35

I t took longer than usual for Aiden to fall asleep. He was a little anxious about bringing the Sleepers into his dream. The Sleepers had their hopes up and were all counting on him. *This better work.*

He closed his eyes and focused on his friends, picturing their faces one at a time. Fitz with his unibrow. Lax, the gentle giant. Hal, the freckled-face kid genius whose ears and cheeks were always the same shade of pink. Farmer, Hispanic like him but with a much lighter complexion. To him, she was like a flower, a rose-bud opening to reveal its increasing beauty each day. He pictured the armful of bracelets she always wore. There was something about those beads. He reminded himself to ask her about them again.

He pictured Quest, the Nigerian, music lover, one day interstellar traveler. Tristan the brave, whose haircut reminded him of James Dean—a low fade with the top brushed up and combed over to the side. Oui, the scientific one, whose hacking obsession reminded him a lot of Coulter, except that Oui was Caucasian with a spiky faux hawk. Bale, the commander in the making that always stuffed his face with food as if he would never eat again. And lastly, Danai.

He focused on her face the longest. Her loose curls, her full lips, her dimple, and her olive skin, flawless except for a single mole just above her collar bone. He thought about her arched eyebrows, how one always raised higher than the other, and how you could hardly tell her eyes were open when she laughed. He was surprised how detailed he was about her features compared to the others.

As he began to drift off, he saw a single curly strand of her hair with sunlight shining through it against a blue sky.

Within seconds, he stood on the Golden Gate Bridge, looking to the east over the San Francisco Bay. He looked to his right as Danai walked toward him, her hair blowing in the wind just as he had envisioned it. A strapless white gown flowed around her. In his dream, she almost floated toward him rather than walked.

She abruptly stopped smiling. "Exactly why am I wearing this?"

"Oh, sorry. Not sorry." Aiden said with a sly grin. *Did I really just say that?*

In the blink of an eye, her attire changed. He noticed Danai looking past him at Farmer. She smiled with her usual crooked smile, which Aiden thought added to her looks. Halland appeared next, followed by the rest of the Sleepers. They were all dressed alike in black jumpsuits because Aiden saw them as a team.

"This is cool," said Bale while pointing across the water at Alcatraz.

Oui enthusiastically patted him on the arm. "You did it, kid. We're all here."

"We just have to check in and make sure we all remember it in the morning. What year is this? Can we jump?" Lax asked. He climbed up onto the rail.

"Get back down here," Quest demanded while pulling him down.

Halland pointed at Aiden. "It's *his* dream. That means our abilities and anything we do here are up to him."

"What year *is* this?" asked Tristan. "It looks different."

"Twenty-ten."

"Cool."

"Twenty-ten? Is it a dream or are we actually here?" asked Bale.

Aiden opened his mouth to speak.

Quest put his hand up. "I got this. Does everyone here dream in color?"

They all nodded.

"Good. So everyone sees all the beauty of the San Francisco Bay that I'm seeing right now. Does everyone feel the moisture in the wind?"

They agreed.

"How about the rail?"

Everyone grabbed it.

"The cars? Can you hear the traffic, the sound of their engines and their wheels rolling over the bridge, the music blasting from some of them, those that yell at us, or beep their horns? Do you smell the ocean?"

"Yeah, so where is this going?" asked Lax.

"When you dream, you usually only have one other sense along with sight. You may or may not feel the air or the ground under you. Things just exist. If you taste something, you may not feel a touch, or if you feel pain you don't smell anything. You may see, hear, and feel a touch if your mind is that active, but that is usually the extent of it. You don't feel your presence or have a sense of being. It's like watching a movie. You can see and hear it, but that's the extent of the experience. Am I right?"

"Quest is right. It doesn't get any realer than this," said Bale.

Aiden noticed Fitz looked uneasy, like he might throw up. "Are you okay?"

"Yeah, it's just the height. I'll be fine."

"More proof that this is really happening. Did you know Fitz was afraid of heights, Aiden?" asked Bale.

"I'm not afraid, I just don't like it."

"No, I didn't know. Sorry about that, Fitz."

"Okay, kids," said Oui, "Enough with the chit chat. Now that we are all here, what are we going to do?"

"Let me get this straight," interrupted Tristan. "We are actually back in time in twenty-ten because our dreams become reality, so we are actually time traveling right now."

Some looked surprised they hadn't thought of that, and others nodded.

"So," he continued, "Because you didn't dream us into an imaginary place, anything of significance we do should appear in the news or something."

"I guess. This is new to me too," Aiden replied.

"If you hurt someone or even one of us gets hurt, is it really happening?" asked Bale. "Scratch that first part. I think we all know what can happen to others, but will we Sleepers really have those injuries?"

That revelation changed everyone's countenance. A few looked concerned.

"But," said Farmer. Everyone looked in her direction, always surprised to hear her speak up. She was interrupted by a semi-truck that for some reason blew its horn at them as it passed. She continued. "If you dream someone is healed, will they be healed? If you dream that I am no longer a Sleeper, will I no longer have this ability?" She looked hopeful.

Tristan stepped forward. He too was curious.

Aiden paced back and forth with his hand under his chin. "I wish I had all the answers, but I don't. That's what these experiments are for, answers.

"We know that what we do to others sticks," he kept his head turned away from Lax, "but what we do to other Sleepers, I don't know. We will find out together."

Aiden had an idea. "Someone needs to volunteer to cut himself. When you wake up, we will know how much my dream affected you. One of you cut yourself. The other I will imagine receiving a cut."

Two hands slowly raised.

A blade appeared in Tristan's right hand. He made a small incision on his left palm. The blade disappeared as he held his hand to clot the blood. Aiden then caused a cut to appear on Oui's hand.

"Next, we need to know if we still have our abilities when we are in the dreams of others. That would make us so much more powerful. You can each try to shake this bridge to see if you can affect my dream. If not, I'll have to give you that power. In the news for this date, it will appear as an earthquake." Aiden noticed Fitz's eyes. "It will be okay, man." He pointed to an area on land. "Do you want to go over there? I can place you there."

"No, we are all facing fears here. I'll try."

The bridge shifted as if a wave ran through it. All the cars screeched to a halt. The Sleepers held fast to the rail. Fitz looked as though he would collapse.

"That was me," said Aiden. "Who's next?"

"I'll go." Quest turned away from the bay and toward the bridge. Everyone waited.

"Nothing happened."

"I don't think it will," said Halland. "Aiden, it's your dream, so whatever we do is because you allow it."

"Try again," Aiden instructed Quest. The bridge shifted again. They all yelled out as the bridge stopped moving.

"Yeah!" exclaimed Bale with his fist in the air. "Me next." He repeated what Quest had done.

"Farmer, you go," said Aiden. She too was successful.

"My turn," said Lax. He looked out at the water east of them toward the Gulf of Farallones. The water became choppier. Large waves were building and lapping hard against the shore. It was as if the sea had been asleep and angrily awoke, thrashing about uncontrollably.

Is he doing that? Aiden looked at Lax.

People began to get out of their vehicles and look out toward the ocean.

Danai tapped Aiden hard on the back.

Aiden turned toward the bay to see what Danai was pointing at. The water in the bay was receding. He turned back around, and his mouth dropped. In the distance, it looked as though a grey mountainous land mass was ahead of them, but it was growing in height and nearing them. A wave was building—a tidal wave.

"What are you doing?" Tristan yelled at Lax as the wave rose.

"Lax, stop," Aiden yelled.

The wave looked to have reached a hundred feet. "Do something," said Bale.

Farmer flung her hands up over her mouth.

"Back down," Aiden said softly.

Sea water rushed back into the bay as the wave descended. Lax turned to Aiden, irritated that his test had been interrupted.

"What the heck is with you and water," Aiden yelled at him.

Lax lunged toward him.

"Wake up," said Aiden, just before Lax's body collided with his.

Everyone disappeared from the bridge except for Aiden.

Emergency sirens blared from every direction. *How did everything just go left like that?* He watched the frenzy as people fled their vehicles. Some cars tried to drive around other cars to get off the bridge. It was no use. The bridge was gridlocked.

Out of everything he'd witnessed, the terror he saw in the eyes of a little girl on a school bus was the most disturbing. Aiden could feel how frightened she was and how much she wanted her parents as he slowly began to fade.

CHAPTER 36

A iden rose early to meet the Sleepers at breakfast. Lax sat alone at a table. Aiden took a seat across from him, and he looked up.

"Lax, I'm sorry, man. I really didn't mean to bring up the whole water thing with Lurssen. I'm stupid. Chalk it up to that."

"I wasn't going to hurt anyone," Lax replied as Halland sat next to him.

Halland noticed Aiden didn't have a tray in front of him. "Aren't you going to eat?"

"Nah, I can't eat. Too much going on in here," Aiden replied while pointing at his head.

Halland leaned forward. "We have to remember that whatever we do in a real place will show up in the news. You were creating something catastrophic," he charged Lax. "It could have gone very wrong. I wonder if it was in the news."

"Believe me," said Aiden, "the triple threat is already on it."

He spoke of Tristan, Quest, and Oui. The three walked in as if they were summoned and rushed to the table.

"We made the news—back then," Oui stated excitedly.

"Shh . . ."

Oui lowered his voice. "The report stated an earthquake caused a tsunami effect, but that it quickly subsided. There's video footage and photos from people on the bridge."

"How do you know it was from us?" asked Lax.

"You're not going to believe this . . . We're in the footage."

CHAPTER 37

A iden walked down the hall of the medical building, looking behind him every few feet.

Is Funky Girl following me?

He had just left organic chemistry and noticed Ms. Funky in the hall. She acted peculiar, not looking away when he looked at her, but staring hard at him with a blank expression. It reminded him of the man in his building that day.

More students entered the hall from a door on the right as their class released. Aiden quickly dodged through the bodies and raced down the hall. *Let's see if she follows me.*

Aiden turned the corner. "Whoa!" He grabbed Farmer as they collided. She had been coming around the corner from the opposite direction at the same time.

"Good catch," she said with an uncomfortable laugh as she steadied herself and let go of his arms.

"You okay?" asked Aiden.

"Yeah. I guess I have too much on my mind."

"Same here. Where are you headed?"

"That way." She pointed down the corridor Aiden had just exited from. He could see Ms. Funky's afro off to the side. The area cleared quickly as she leaned against the wall, watching them. Farmer began to walk away.

"Wait. You got a minute?"

She stopped walking and looked over her shoulder. "Sure, what's up?"

"Farmer, do you really want to change who you are?"

"Why do you ask that?"

"Your question about—"

"Oh, last night."

"Yeah."

She stared off to the right.

Aiden was just about to touch her. She had become so still for so long. Then she spoke. "If you could live a normal life, or there was a possibility that you could, wouldn't you try? Wouldn't you like to sleep in a normal bed and read or watch whatever you want? Wouldn't you want your dreams to be harmless depictions of your anxieties or fears or a result of whatever meal you ate too close to bedtime, if it would keep people safe?"

Farmer looked into his eyes when she said the last part. Hers filled with tears to the brim, but they held as if they refused to be released. He didn't realize how much pain she carried with her until that moment.

They stood, fixated on each other. Aiden couldn't bring himself to break from her gaze. There was something there, deep in her eyes.

"Aiden," yelled Halland from down the hall.

"Ahem." Aiden cleared his throat. "I, uh, I'll see you later," he said. He quickly turned and rushed toward Halland. He couldn't think. He felt warm, and his heart raced. *What is happening?*

CHAPTER 38

Minutes passed like hours as the Sleepers sat through each class, waiting to meet up and discuss their dream experiment. Finally, they stood in Oui's room, staring at the display wall at an image of the Golden Gate Bridge with them on it. There wasn't just one photo, there were many with the same hashtag from that day, #goldengatequake.

Aiden gritted his teeth, annoyed. "See, this is what cannot happen. Anything we do cannot be traced back to us. We must be undetected."

"I noticed something else. I don't think anyone else paid attention," said Fitz.

"What did you see?"

"The sky changed according to Aiden's mood. When he was happy, it was a bright sunny sky. There were times when it became grey and when he saw the wave, clouds began to swarm in."

"Wow, really?" asked Aiden.

"Yeah."

"That's exactly what these experiments are for. Fitz, we'll expect you to always notice the things we may not be focused on, like our surroundings."

Fitz nodded with a look of accomplishment. "Who's next tonight?"

Lax and Farmer both said, "Me," at the same time.

"Ladies first," said Lax as he rose to leave. He glanced at Aiden, and then back at Farmer and left.

Aiden sighed. "He's still angry."

"Who cares, he was wrong. Look, I've been thinking," said Quest. "If we go to a place that doesn't really exist, where are we exactly? Somewhere floating in time? We can't be in the person's mind, can we?"

"Okay, this is getting too deep. Let's stick with places that exist. Farmer, you know what to do, right?"

She nodded. "Focus on each of you before bed."

Aiden smiled. "Yes, but take us to a place less menacing."

CHAPTER 39

I nside his dorm suite, Aiden ran his hand over a panel. His kitchen unit unfolded as it extended out of the wall. He placed a flat, rectangular piece of metal, no larger than his hand, on the counter. He pressed the top and it flipped up, a piece under that flipped down, and two pieces opened out to the sides, causing the whole object to triple in size. Once fully opened, yellow, green, red, and blue bars rose and fell over the display panel. The bottom area became a keyboard, but with only dots and no letters or numbers.

The gadget was Coulter's latest invention and totally undetectable. Aiden found it inside the clothing Ms. Genova had brought back from his mother. He wasn't surprised his mother had snuck it in after what had happened. Ms. Genova visiting his home, though? That was the weird part. Maybe she and his mother had made amends. *Hmph, not likely.*

Aiden made notes on everything he'd discovered. How all the Sleepers joined him in his dream, which they now termed a visionscope because of the line they crossed between a dream and reality, the revelation from Fitz, how they could use their abilities after being allowed by the visioner, and how Oui's scar remained after he awoke. An injury to a Sleeper would only remain if the visioner, the person having the dream, caused it.

He also made note of what Lax had done. It was odd and very unlike Lax's normal happy-go-lucky personality.

Now, how do I keep this hidden? Aiden couldn't be certain that whoever was running the Institute couldn't retrieve everything they typed.

Where would it be safe? He couldn't send it to his mother. After her showing up at the Institute, someone was probably looking into everything about her and hacking into her system.

There was only one person he trusted other than his mother, and he was the only person whose system would alert him if anyone tried to find a backdoor in. *Coulter.*

Coulter didn't know Aiden's secret. Aiden wasn't even sure how to tell him without sounding like a complete lunatic. He typed a letter.

Coulter,

Hey man, first I want to apologize for being MIA, but I know it would take a lot more than that to ruin our friendship. At least, I hope so. And if we are as tight as I think we are, what I'm going to tell you won't ruin it either.

You and I, we have no secrets, except for one. It's the real reason I stayed home from school on those days when you came to pick me up. I have a condition, and there is no cure. I am called a Sleeper. Whatever I dream comes to life. You probably think I mean metaphorically. No, that's literal. I'm talking a giant anaconda slithering around my room while I'm dreaming about it. I know it sounds unreal, but think about the damage to my home you've seen getting repaired over the years. It's also the reason I could never attend one of your gamer-fest sleepovers.

It's real, Coulter. If I dream it, it happens.

You probably wonder why I'm telling you now. Things are getting weird here at the Institute. Take a look at the attached file. I really need your help, Coult. You can verify all of this with my mom.

A.

He knew Coulter. His friend had to believe him.

CHAPTER 40

COULTER

Coulter dropped into a chair that looked like it was about to take off in flight. With a cookie hanging out of his mouth, he strapped himself in and donned a pair of flat holo-goggles. Music roared through the room. That's the way he liked to work on things. The chair rose four feet into the air and angled back, positioning Coulter so he was looking up at the ceiling.

Having rich parents enabled his hacker's dream room. His entire bedroom turned into the inside of a central processing unit for controlling and executing operations. With his goggles on, only he could see the files and coding that opened and closed on the walls and ceiling around the room as he maneuvered the chair in every direction.

As he bobbed his head to the music, an alert flashed in front of him. *What's that?* An encrypted message was sent to his secret address—the one he only shared with other hackers.

Coulter opened the message and began reading. He bit down on the cookie, which dropped from his mouth onto his chest. The piece that was in his mouth, he spit off to the side.

"What the— Is he kidding me? Not funny, Aiden. Let me see . . ."

The chair spun to the right. Coulter used that area to display images along the wall, as well as information on the Institute of Anomalous Intelligence. He spun to the left, sending an encrypted message to his hacker friends that had a higher skill set for the type of digging he required.

Within minutes, he began to receive images and articles about Sleepers. He punched his fist into his hand. "This is big. Bigger than—It must be government." He thought for a moment. *Or terrorists.*

His fingers went to work on the holoboard. He needed to find a backdoor to get into the Institute's mainframe. He attached a sensor to the left and right sides of his head, making it possible to manipulate the chair without using his hands. He tilted his head, and the chair turned to the back wall, where he raised his hands and pulled and pushed information he would need forward or off to the side as he found it. He found a backdoor into a government information system and typed in Aiden's last name. His eyes widened as he watched someone in an undisclosed location searching the same name.

CHAPTER 41

It's interesting how your mind can be so exhausted from thinking that it tires you physically, Aiden thought as he laid back into the soft cushion of his sleep chamber. Before it could self-adjust to his body weight, he was asleep.

Aiden opened his eyes and looked around at a field. The most vibrant shade of blue butterflies rested on the plants before him—thousands of them, almost creating a blanket of blue over the foliage. Cuarto guitars were being played from somewhere nearby. The temperature was nice and warm, with a slight breeze that blew a hint of cilantro through the air. Someone prepared dinner in a home at the bottom of the hill.

"The place is real, but the butterflies are yours," said Aiden.

Farmer's voice met his ear. "How did you know?"

"Your tattoo."

She smiled and looked away as the rest of the team appeared.

"Okay, this is what we are going to do. Each one of us will manipulate these butterflies as soon as Farmer allows us our ability," Aiden said, nodding at her.

She nodded back.

"You first, Danai."

Danai stepped forward. The butterflies rose into the air at once and flew around them, landing on their arms, shoulders, heads, and noses. They all smiled as they watched. Halland flinched a little, as though he were going to get bitten, before relaxing.

"You go, Bale."

The butterflies flew out in front of them and began to swirl together in a circle. Before they knew it, a thick wall of butterflies swirled around them, as if they stood in the center of a cylinder of blue waves.

"Nice." Aiden tried to sound upbeat, although he wasn't sure he should move on to Lax. "Your turn, Lax."

The butterflies dispersed all around them, settling back on the foliage. The sky became grey as a light mist of rain turned into a drizzle. Aiden's head snapped toward Lax.

"Seriously," yelled Fitz at Lax.

"Calm down. It was just a joke."

The rain stopped. Tristan and Fitz, standing on either side of Lax, both reached over and knocked him in the arm.

He frowned. "Seriously though, what do I look like out here playing around with butterflies?"

Farmer walked over to him and wrapped her arm through his. "Someone who understands that in order to become more than he is, he has to investigate every theory about himself and continue learning." She smiled at him, her eyes shining brightly.

Lax raised his hand and a butterfly landed on it. It immediately morphed into a flower of the same vibrant blue hues.

Farmer took the flower from his hand and smiled, then walked back toward Aiden and winked at him in passing as she placed the flower in her hair. For the first time, Lax was at a loss for words.

"Lax showed us something new," said Aiden. "He changed something Farmer created. Let's remember to make note of that. Now I think it's time we all get some proper rest."

Before Farmer woke them, Aiden walked over and whispered to Lax, "I didn't know you were such a gentleman."

"I'm a lot more than you think."

CHAPTER 42

T he next night was Lax's turn to bring them all into his visionscope. Aiden dreaded entering it. Something was happening with Lax. The glimmer in his eye, usually always there no matter what, was gone and replaced with a hardened stare. He'd grown quiet and easily agitated. He and Aiden had become close, but now he distanced himself from Aiden.

Aiden laid back and focused hard on Lax. Sleep finally found him, but he awoke half an hour later still in his chamber. *What's going on? Is Lax not asleep yet?* He sighed and fought to keep his mind from wandering from Lax or the others so Lax could bring him in.

Danai looked around. All the Sleepers appeared on a railway in the middle of nowhere. "Could we at least have jackets? It's freezing out here. Where are we?" she asked as she crossed her arms in front of her and shivered.

"You will know soon enough. I want to show you what I can do," Lax replied.

"You brought us here so you could show off?" asked Oui. "That's not the purpose of these experiments."

They could hear a train approaching in the distance and turned, watching it round the bend. "Is it me or is that train traveling way too fast?" asked Tristan.

Halland stepped forward, briskly rubbing his arms for warmth. "Yeah, it is."

Bale's head twisted in the opposite direction. "There's another one coming. What are you doing, Lax?"

Danai looked back and forth from the trains to Lax, becoming more fearful by the second. Farmer stood at her side. "Where's Aiden?"

"The party-poop? He'll be here eventually."

Concern covered the girls' faces as both trains roared closer, continuing to pick up speed.

Tristan nudged Oui. "We have to do something," he whispered.

"Lax, this is not safe!" Oui exclaimed.

"Okay, sheesh." An electrified force shot from Lax's hand and onto the tracks of the second train, slowing it down.

The Sleepers were yelling, but he couldn't hear what they were saying due to the train's rails screeching and horns sounding.

The first train came up too fast. The cars lurched and flipped on the track. Danai screamed. They looked up, seeing a car of the train in the air directly above their heads. Lax turned too late to see what was happening, and he hadn't thought to give the others the ability to make changes in his visionscope. Three of the train cars twisted and crashed into the ravine, followed by a huge explosion.

CHAPTER 43

There are two sounds you never forget, the sound of metal smashing and scraping against metal, and the violent roar of an explosion.

Lax ran toward the wreckage, but the force of the blast threw him back onto the ground. Crawling away from the blaze, he screamed, "Fitz! Tristan!" He continued crying out for the others as he stood. "Halland! Farmer!"

A blue light above the blaze glimmered through the smoke. Farmer's bracelets. The Sleepers floated in the air above the wreckage.

"How are we up here?" asked Quest.

Halland pointed. "Look!"

Aiden stood a distance away with his arms outstretched toward them. He guided them closer and lowered them to the ground.

"How did you—" Quest ran to him and wrapped his arms around him, lifting off his feet. "Aiden, you can enter someone's dream without being invited and manipulate the dream without them giving you access?"

Everyone watched him in wonder.

Lax's expression filled with shock and shame.

"This was planned by Lax and me to try something new, test our limits," Aiden said, walking around them.

Lax's head rose.

"We didn't know if it would work, but as you can see, it did. We know something new about us now."

"Something new about *you*," said Fitz.

"Yeah, the rest of us can't do this," Bale added. "I tried as soon as I saw that second train approaching."

Passengers began to emerge from the train and helped the injured. Aiden watched them. "Don't worry, they can't see us. Lax has put up a wall. We are invisible to them. Good job stopping the other train, Lax."

"Won't this be in the news?" asked Danai.

"This incident already happened, but for different reasons. Lax researched the accident before bringing you here."

"Wake up," whispered Lax.

Everyone disappeared except he and Aiden.

"Can we die here?"

"I don't know, but it's better to think we can so we take the necessary precautions."

"I—I don't know what to say."

"You don't have to say anything." Aiden held out his fist to him. "Are we good?"

Lax raised his fist and then opened his hand.

Aiden, surprised, took his hand and they shook. No one shook hands anymore due to a pandemic years ago.

The smile that had begun to form on Aiden's face quickly subsided. They both looked down at their hands.

"Did you feel that? What was that?" asked Lax.

Aiden shook his head. "I don't know. Quick, bring everyone back in."

The Sleepers reappeared in the same location, but the people and trains were gone.

"I thought we were done for the night," Halland fussed.

"Me too. I've had enough for one visionscope," Fitz complained.

Aiden and Lax stood side by side. "Fitz, take Bale's hand," said Lax.

"We don't take hands," Bale responded.

"We're in a visionscope. Just do it."

Bale reluctantly reached for Fitz's hand. Aiden and Lax waited for their reaction. "Well?"

"Well, what? Why am I holding his hand?" asked Bale as he shoved it away.

"This is weird," Danai mumbled.

"What's going on?" asked Tristan.

"Aiden, maybe it's you." said Lax. "Someone, take Aiden's hand."

"What do you mean, maybe it's him?" asked Quest, intrigued. He stepped forward on the opposite side of Aiden and took his hand.

Quest jumped. "Whoa! What was that?"

"Aiden must be the anchor. Everyone, grab someone's hand," Lax exclaimed.

Lax and Quest stood on either side of Aiden. As each Sleeper joined them, they jumped, feeling the flow of energy through their bodies.

The ten of them stood in a circle, looking at each other, fascinated by what was happening. A soft light surrounded them.

"What is happening?" Farmer whispered barely loud enough for anyone to hear.

"It's getting stronger," yelled Halland as he began to back away.

"No!" yelled Oui. "Don't break the bond!"

Halland stepped forward again.

"What does this mean?" said Aiden. A high-pitched ringing began in their ears, followed by the sound of something exploding from a tight container.

They all disappeared from where they were standing.

CHAPTER 44

Aiden awoke in his sleep chamber feeling more rested than he had in a long time. He thought of the Sleepers' encounter the night before. *That was wild.* He climbed out of his chamber feeling different somehow, renewed.

I wonder if I look different. He slapped his belly. *Flat stomach, good build, same as usual.* He smiled to himself as he walked to his en-suite mirror. When he saw himself, he jumped back, and then slowly leaned over the sink, bringing his face close to the mirror.

His pupils had changed color, taking on a bright blue hue, but quickly dissipated. He pulled his eyelid up. *What is going on?*

Aiden spotted Quest walking across the quad and ran to catch up to him.

"What'cha got?"

Quest jumped, almost dropping the pod he was drinking from. "Dude, what is up with you?"

"Me? Why are you so jumpy?"

"That thing last night."

"Any clues to what that was?"

"The best I can figure is there is some connection between us as Sleepers. Being together has unleashed something," said Quest. But—"

"But what?"

"It centers around you—like you're the catalyst."

"But we've touched before. Why now?"

"Not like that, we haven't. I'm stuck on that part."

"Hey," Oui yelled as he approached them. "I've been looking for you guys."

Quest filled him in on what they were discussing.

"This may be reaching a bit, but what if we are coming of age or something. We are all the same—"

"Except for Halland," Aiden pointed out.

"Yeah, but that's only in years."

"Did you guys notice anything different when you awoke this morning?" Aiden asked.

"No, why?" asked Oui.

"Nope," Quest replied.

"Just wondering."

"My theory is that being together is making this—whatever it is inside of us—evolve us," Oui said.

Aiden stopped walking. "That's too much. I can't go there right now, and I don't even understand why that doesn't scare you."

"I'm just saying. Something's been dormant or asleep within us. We're something different—different from ordinary Homo sapiens."

"It makes sense, though," said Quest. "It may just be me, but I think things are about to start changing in our waking lives. Except for you, maybe?"

"Why would you say that?" Aiden asked, surprised.

"I wasn't sure at first, but now I'm certain. You've been talking to us in our heads all along."

"No, I haven't. That's not possible."

"Yeah, you have," Oui agreed. "Asleep or awake, we've heard you."

CHAPTER 45

The next Sleeper meeting took place at Fitz's chess competition. A holographic, cube-shaped chess board floated in the air on a diagonal in front of the players as they manipulated the pieces on every side.

"What have we learned so far, other than the fact that we are changing?" Quest asked.

"Remember, we only discuss that changing theory in visionscopes from here on out," Aiden reminded them.

"We've learned how fear limits us. It blocks your ability in someone else's visionscope. We saw that when Tristan brought in Fitz," Bale said.

Fitz looked away. Aiden shook his shoulder. "Hey, it's cool. We know you were nervous. That's why we're doing this. To find out what we are capable of."

Halland laughed. "We learned that Lax is a psycho."

No one made a sound, nor cracked a smile. Aiden closed his eyes, pursed his lips, and slowly shook his head. Lax turned to Halland, his lips curled in a snarl, and leaned toward him.

Halland instantly hushed. "Too soon?"

Aiden nodded.

"Hal," growled Lax while leaning over him like a grizzly bear over a puppy. "Don't make me change my mind about liking you."

"I didn't mean—I apologize for that." Hal pointed at his head. "Sometimes I begin talking before I think, and it causes a conflict between my brain and my mouth. And then I just run off like a faucet. It has to do with the stratum function of my cerebral cortex—the gray matter, really—"

"Dude, shut up," Bale exclaimed.

Everyone burst into laughter.

"Okay, well, we've learned that Halland, the baby of the family here," Aiden said as he patted his back, "rambles when he's nervous. Please, whatever you do, don't make him nervous."

"Look, I'm up next, so fill me in later," Fitz stated as he stood. The Sleepers rose also. "Where are you going? Stay right there and cheer me on."

"Seriously? Who cheers at a chess tournament?" asked Quest.

"And this thing could last longer than a baseball game or Wimbledon!" added Tristan.

"Support. It's Sleeper code, remember?" joked Fitz while walking backward.

"No, it's not, but hey, we'll consider adding it after your tournament." Aiden chuckled. He looked over at Oui, who sat typing away at something. He had been silent throughout the whole meeting.

"What are you working on?" Aiden asked as he sat next to him.

"It's a surprise." He looked up, searching the group, and found Quest. Their eyes locked. They shared some secret that Aiden didn't feel like prying into.

"Hey, where are the girls?" asked Halland.

"They're with Brooks," Lax replied.

Aiden spun around. "Brooks? Why?"

"She says she wants to get to know them and all of you."

Aiden stood. "Why? What have you told her?"

"Nothing. She just wants to know my friends," Lax replied defensively while stepping toward Aiden.

Bale stepped between them. "Not in here. Take this outside."

Aiden and Lax stood in the courtyard under a tree with Bale, Quest, Tristan, Oui, and Halland surrounding them.

"I'm missing something. What's the problem?" asked Tristan.

"The problem is, he doesn't trust anyone that isn't a Sleeper. Oh, anyone other than his idol, Dr. Laribe. Am I the only one that has friends who aren't Sleepers?" asked Lax.

Quest said, "No, we all have other friends."

"Exactly. So why is Brooks the one you have a problem with?"

Aiden didn't want to tell them he felt Brooks clung to Lax too much, Lax talked too much and was probably telling her everything, and that she could be the enemy or reporting back to someone. That could be said of any of their friends that weren't Sleepers, but his issue was with Brooks. She was always around, in their faces, being nosey, trying to hear as much as she could. He couldn't put his finger on it, but something wasn't right with her.

"I don't have an issue with her," he said. "I just want you to be careful—everyone to be careful—about what you say to anyone who isn't a Sleeper. Especially those that you get close to. That's all. We don't know what's going on here yet."

"My girl isn't part of this!" Lax stepped closer to Aiden's face. Tristan pulled him away from Aiden.

"Hey, hey. Disagreements are normal, but let's not forget, we're a team. We don't fight each other," Aiden said.

"You're right, but speaking against her will only push them closer together," Quest whispered toward Aiden.

"That's Sleeper code," Tristan continued.

"No, it's not," said Bale. "But let's make it so and add it to what is already code." He looked from Lax to Aiden. "We don't talk to anyone about anything that involves being a Sleeper, and we don't fight each other. Agreed?"

"Agreed," both Lax and Aiden stated. Aiden looked away, but he could still feel Lax's eyes burning into him.

"Speaking of Sleeper code—actually, I think what I'm about to say has more to do with Sleeper morals—we are not to use our ability for make-out sessions," said Aiden.

"Freaking Danai," Oui said under his breath, looking away.

Lax put his hand up to his mouth and jumped up and down, laughing. "No way! Who did that?"

"She tells everything," said Tristan.

Oui sighed. "We get it. She broke it down for us. The girls will wake up feeling violated."

"Yeah, as if they were raped, and that's not who we are," Aiden said.

Tristan waved his hands in front of his face. "No, it was strictly PG. No R rated stuff."

Lax chuckled, and then became straight-faced while wagging his index finger at them like a disappointed parent. "Get your girls the old-fashioned way. That's one for the Sleeper code, moral, or whatever."

"Now we just need a Sleeper handshake or something," said Halland.

Lax playfully put Halland in a headlock. "What are we, eight like you?"

CHAPTER 46

MRS. QUINN

An automated call from the administrative office of the Institute explained the new school media network app, which allowed the students to update their statuses daily.

Parents could log in and keep up with what's happening on campus. They were informed that the app was Ms. Genova's idea, and its creation and implementation had been expedited per her request.

Mrs. Quinn logged in daily to view Aiden's status, which he rarely updated. Occasionally there was something about his workouts, his meeting with his mentor, Dr. Laribe, events he attended with his friends, or exams.

Mrs. Quinn read today's status aloud. "Checking high-end Chinese kites or urchin tables tomorrow early as can hack every retailer. Hopefully on Utah site easier rates."

Huh? She stared at the post for a few minutes rubbing her forehead. *What the heck is he talking about? It makes no sense. Why would he—? Wait a minute, wait a minute. This can't be him. I know she didn't—*

Mrs. Quinn grabbed a stylus and circled the first letter of each word. *Yes, she did. Amateur. CHECK OUT TEACHER HOUSER.*

She was pleased to find the site was set up so that after viewing the status, the update disappeared into the messaging crypt, never to be seen again, and could not be retrieved.

She'd met Professor Houser. He didn't seem the type to be involved in a government coverup. But then, you never really knew anyone.

Call from Coulter."

"Put him through."

She could hear him breathing. "You're on the air."

"Huh? Mrs. Quinn? This is Coulter."

She laughed. "Yes, I know that, Coulter. How are you?"

"Good, I'm good. Um . . . I know Aiden is not around, so you may not take the breaks away from your work that you used to . . ."

There was a long pause. Mrs. Quinn leaned forward in her seat. "Coulter?"

"I'm here." He sighed heavily. "I guess what I'm trying to say is would you like to go to the movies? Oh, that was a question. What I should have said was what I'm trying to ask, because—"

"Coulter!"

"Ma'am?"

"Aiden asked you to check on me, didn't he?"

Coulter was silent.

"It's okay, I won't tell him you told me."

"Yes, ma'am. He asked me to, but I would have done it anyway."

"I'm sure you would have," she said as she rolled her eyes. "I have a deposition I'm preparing for, but I will need a break at some point. What do you have in mind and when?"

"There's a retro marathon at Carnival."

"Carnival? You want me to go there, as old as I am? Only kids hang out there."

"No, not just kids, but you'll have the fun I imagine you work too hard to have. So are you in?" he asked, sounding unsure of himself.

Is he calling me a workaholic? "I'm in. What time?"

"Tomorrow at seven. Don't eat. I mean eat, of course, but leave room for food too."

The call disconnected. *All the book smarts in the world, but not a lick of common sense at all.*

CHAPTER 47

Aiden noticed the same two students occupied the same two seats at the front of economics class, and they always looked back at him, watching.

He sat drumming his fingers on his table. *Five more minutes and I'm going.* He'd determined the best way to get back to the hallway on the first floor of the dormitory without rousing suspicion would be to go when he was expected to be in class. Not once had he noticed anyone entering or exiting that area since the day he and Danai saw the man walk through the wall.

If what Danai said was correct, maybe the wall was never solid, and he could just walk right through. Since they didn't have to scan to enter the dorm, no one would know he was there instead of in class.

Aiden excused himself and glanced over his shoulder. One of the guys at the front of the class motioned to the other, who put his hand up and shook his head as if to say, it's okay, let him go. At least that's how Aiden interpreted it.

Outside the classroom, he looked up and down the corridor, noticing how still everything seemed, like an abandoned building. No one was in the other classes. However, they always flooded the hall when the bell rang, signaling the end of the period. *Where could everyone be?* he thought.

He stepped into the restroom, passed by the urinal stalls to reach the window, and looked outside. No students or instructors walked the grounds. It seemed as still and empty as the interior.

Shrubs formed a hedge just below the window. *Those should break my fall. Now to get the window open.* The frame was an old mechanism no longer used.

He grabbed the knob. *How does this work?* He pushed and pulled it up and down. It moved a little, but nothing happened. He stared at the brass knob for a moment before grabbing the handle and turning it. The window opened to the outside, but not very far—just enough for him to squeeze through and stumble into the soil behind the shrubs. Peeking over the shrubs and seeing that no one saw him, he ran toward the dormitory. *Did they evacuate the campus? No one's out here.*

"This doesn't look like a restroom to me," a familiar voice behind him stated.

Aiden stopped walking and turned to face the speaker. It was Halland. "Kid, what are you doing in here?"

"Don't *kid* me. My voice is as deep as yours, and I'm in the same grade you're in, so that makes us equal."

"First of all, you're twelve."

Halland rolled his eyes. "Mentally, I'm thirty. What's second?"

"Second . . ." Aiden's voice trailed off as he looked to the side. "You're right. Your voice is deep. How the heck did that happen?"

"I've been drinking hater juice," Halland smirked.

"Get back to class. I'll be there in a minute."

"Were you married to my mother? I mean, you don't look like my dad. So if you're not, I will go where I choose and right now, I choose to follow—"

Footsteps sounded, and Aiden wrapped his hand around Halland's mouth and pulled him into the alcove of the wall. He held his finger up to his mouth and peeked around the corner. Halland leaned below Aiden and took a quick look. A man walked to the end of the hallway and right through the wall, just as the other one had that day when he was with Danai. *She was right. That wall is never solid. What are they hiding?*

Aiden leaned back out of sight. "I'm going to take a look. You stay here. I mean it, Hal." He could see in Halland's eyes that he was equally fascinated.

"Not on your life. If that's what I think it is, you're going to need my intelligence just to understand what's happening on the other side of that vortex energy field."

Aiden eyes widened. *Is that what it's called? This kid is too smart for his own good.* "Come on, then."

They quickly walked to the end of the hall. Aiden glanced behind him every few steps in case someone entered the corridor, all the while trying to think up an excuse as to why they would be there.

They stopped directly in front of the wall. "There could be people on the other side waiting for us."

"Or there could be the other end of this hall." Halland glanced at Aiden, then back at the wall.

"Let's do it together."

Halland eyes filled with both fear and excitement.

Aiden reassured him. "We're a team, we're in this together. If we get caught, I'm going to say you brought me here." He smirked. "On three." Aiden glanced over his shoulder one last time to make sure no one was coming. "One. Two." He closed his eyes and pushed Halland through by the shoulder.

CHAPTER 48

T he vortex energy field couldn't have been more than an inch thick. Cold swirls of energy surrounded Aiden like waves of heavy static. He and Halland quickly stepped through it.

"Whew, that was weird. What happened to three?" Halland whispered as he opened his eyes and looked out ahead of them.

Aiden's mouth opened, but he couldn't respond. His eyes darted left and right, up and down, taking in everything. They stood before a suspended walkway that went on from the vast open chamber through a long tunnel-like area. From the left and right of them, the walkway curved out into huge arcs. Lights sparkled from below like New York City at night, revealing various floors of an underground facility.

"What is this?" asked Halland in a whisper, unable to draw his eyes away from the lower levels.

"It's not a school, that's for sure." Aiden pulled Halland away from the railing before he could be seen and motioned for him to follow to the right. A door slid back, and they ducked into the room.

"This looks like a data storage lab," said Halland. "My dad's building has one. His assistant took me on a tour once to keep me occupied while he was in a conference—" Halland abruptly stopped speaking due to the look Aiden shot him.

The room was dimly lit and filled with long plexiglass partitions that hung from the ceiling. "These house data," Halland explained. "A technician types in the air in front of the glass, and the information he needs appears."

Aiden walked up to one of the panels as data scrolled downward. Something caught his eye. He tapped in the air in front of the panel. The data stopped and transmitted a slideshow of footage in front of him showing *Test Subject Alpha Ten*.

"He probably doesn't even know," said Halland, joining him in front of the partition.

Lax lay in a capsule. The output showed ERRATIC SLEEP CYCLE DE-TECTED. An LED display above him in the glass top of his capsule showed images and sounds from a terrorist attack. "They're attempting to program him," said Aiden.

The output then showed his neurological patterns surging out of control. Aiden swiped to the left and read the scientist's notes. "Test Subject Alpha Ten brain function shut down due to medically induced coma. The reversible coma is allowing the brain to heal while also proving there are no sleep patterns during comatic stasis.

"His brain needed to heal? What have they done to him?"

Halland walked over to another partition. "Uh, Aiden, I think you should see this."

Aiden joined him and read the highlighted area. "Weapons Research."

They turned, hearing the hydraulics of the opening door behind them. A technician wearing a blue coverall stood in the entry. "Hey, what are you kids doing in here?" he exclaimed and rushed in.

Aiden grabbed Halland's shirt, dodging partitions, pulling him to the exit at the other end of the room. The tech followed them. They ran out into the corridor toward the walkway.

Two men, also in blue coveralls, came from the opposite direction.

"Stop them," the technician yelled.

The two workers ran forward as Aiden and Halland dashed to the right, around a huge column and toward the railing.

They were directly across from the vortex energy field. However, a ten-story drop to the bottom of the chamber and the suspended walkway cut them off. There was nowhere to run.

"Over the side," Aiden yelled. They quickly climbed over the rail. Aiden's heart pounded louder than any other sound as he looked below them. He couldn't see the bottom, but he could feel a gust of air blowing up toward them. He scanned the area around them, searching for a way out.

The men approached. "Come on boys, you don't want to do that." The one talking held up one hand as if they were going to back off as another ran forward and grabbed at Halland. Aiden held onto the rail with his left hand while using his right to pull Halland away from the guy.

Aiden gasped as Halland's hands released the rail. He lost his footing and fell backwards.

"I can't hold you," Aiden yelled. Halland's shirt slipped from his fingers. "No!"

He didn't want to see his friend falling to his death, but he had to look.

Where did that come from? "Halland!"

Halland looked around at the metal platform that held him, and then up at Aiden while carefully standing. "Jump! It's integrated!"

The men charged toward Aiden. Aiden turned, closed his eyes, and jumped off the rail. He feet landed on something solid. He opened his eyes and continued running forward, yelling the whole time to keep fear from overtaking him.

With every step they took, the platform shot out another piece before their feet landed. They ran straight through the wall, down the hall, and out the back door to the main building.

"In here," Aiden said as the door slid open for the restroom. They leaned back against the wall, breathing heavily.

"No one is going to believe this," said Halland.

Aiden looked down at him. "We have bigger problems than that," he huffed. "We've been seen."

CHAPTER 49

"Has anyone said anything to you? Have you been approached by anyone?" asked Halland as he sat next to Aiden, glancing around the classroom.

Aiden heard Halland, but his focus was on Professor Houser and why he kept looking at them. *There is something weird about him.*

Aiden was beginning to feel that way about almost everyone on campus. "No. They're probably trying to figure out what to do with us. We know too much now."

"But what do we really know? We didn't see much at all."

"We know this is more than just a school and may not even be a school at all."

"I've been thinking about your ability to go where you want in your dreams—"

"No."

"Hear me out. You can make yourself invisible, give yourself the ability to walk through walls, go back to that lab, and explore the whole place." Halland threw his hands in the air as if he had just come up with the greatest idea in the history of mankind.

Aiden eyed him. He was right. However, based on what they'd seen, finding a way to secure their safety was more urgent.

"I know I am only subbing for Professor Orwin, but we can't all talk at the same time during this lecture. Maybe I should let you take over and fill the class in on what you two are discussing over there," said Professor Houser.

Aiden and Halland both sat up straight and faced the professor.

"Good. I have your attention now."

Professor Houser stood at the front of the class lecturing about who-knows-what. It was all just a bunch of noise, as far as Aiden was concerned. He looked from Houser's hair to his clean-shaven face to his broad shoulders to his arms, his jacket too tight over his biceps. *He's not built like any professor I've ever seen.*

Farmer looked back at him from her seat at the front. Maybe to make sure he'd made it to class, maybe to check on him. He didn't smile, mouth, or motion a hello. She faced forward again, and he stared at the back of her head. But he wasn't seeing her, he was seeing right through her.

This was the man that left Lax the message for him to watch the footage on Dubai. He's in on the whole thing. There was nothing Aiden wanted to hear from him other than what was really going on.

He looked down at his desk, deciding that playing their game was the only option to keep him and his friends safe until they found a way out.

"Sleep."

The word snapped Aiden out of his defiant musings.

Professor Houser walked along the front of the room, one hand in the front pocket of his jacket. Everyone paid close attention. Tristan sat up in his seat. Fitz glanced over at Bale.

"The mind is a powerful thing," said Professor Houser. "After decades of research, there are still many mysteries to how it works. For instance, a scent can cause you to recall something from years ago as if it just happened."

He walked down the aisle past each student. "Everyone, close your eyes. Think about your favorite meal. Who likes pizza?"

Hands shot up all over the room.

"With extra cheese . . ."

Students called out their favorite toppings.

"Mmm . . . Think about that glorious cheese that pulls apart as you separate two slices . . ."

Someone laughed. Aiden had to admit, it was hard to think of him as the enemy. *He's a good actor.*

"Can you smell it? Can you taste it? Is your mouth filling with saliva right now in anticipation of that first delectable bite?"

Heads all around the room were nodding.

"See, that's how powerful the mind is. It's as if the pizza were really here." He laughed. "I know what you all will be having for dinner. Now, let's switch gears a little." Professor Houser looked around the room. "Do you dream?"

Aiden leaned forward in his seat. Everyone nodded, even those in the class that did not appear to be Sleepers.

"Interesting enough, dreams can tell you a lot about a person—what their fears are, how they see themselves. Let's get some examples. Who's not afraid?" He smiled. "What did you dream about last night?"

Everyone looked around the room at each other, not wanting to answer.

"Please, don't everyone speak at once," Professor Houser stated after a few seconds. He pointed at Farmer. She told him of a field in Puerto Rico near her grandmother's house.

"Could you see everything in color?"

"Yes," she responded.

"Could you fly?"

"I don't know. I didn't try."

"Many people can fly in their dreams. What about nudity?"

Farmer blushed and looked away. Some of the boys giggled. Lax jokingly raised his hand, and Tristan pulled it back down.

"Don't be embarrassed, you don't have to answer that one. It is believed that dreaming you're naked symbolizes a variety of things in your waking life, such as an issue you need to deal with or a vulnerability."

"I flew naked," Lax blurted out. Everyone laughed. Aiden even cracked a smile.

"Stop it," said Bale. He was always more serious than the others.

Professor Houser pointed at Aiden. "What about you?"

His brows raised. *Was it me he wanted to question all along, or am I just being paranoid? Okay, let's play.* "I stood on a bridge in, uh, New York."

"I had the same dream," Halland blurted out. Aiden shook his head.

Professor Houser's eyes widened. "Really?"

Halland realized the mistake he'd made and tried to clean it up. "I was in London, though, walking across a bridge heading for Big Ben."

Professor Houser moved on. "Scientists are conducting studies right here at the Institute to figure out exactly what happens during REM sleep—when you dream. It's pretty exciting, actually."

He waved his hand over the display wall and a documentary began, showing everything that had taken place in sleep studies of old. The sensors attached to the person in the bed to measure air flow, brain activity, amount of effort to breathe, and the amount of oxygen in the blood.

"Stages four and five of the sleep cycles are what we are most interested in. In stage four, a person sleeps deeply, and there is limited muscle activity. In stage five, there's rapid eye movement, brain waves speed up, and dreaming occurs. Muscles relax, heart rate increases, and breathing becomes rapid and shallow."

A sleeping man appeared on the display, and Professor Houser pointed at his eyes, watching them move back and forth below his lids. "He's dreaming now. This is the part we want to study, exactly what happens to each person when they dream. But not from the outside as we are seeing now, and not just the readings you can see there on the machines. We want to see into their dreams."

They want to see what we see, thought Aiden.

"We already know what happens," whispered Lax. Professor Houser turned and stared at him.

Uh oh. Why did he say that? Aiden watched Professor Houser scratch behind his ear. *Did he just touch an earpiece?* Aiden watched his lips closely.

"They know."

CHAPTER 50

The next day was another long day of classes and labs. Aiden looked over his shoulder everywhere he went, fearing someone might try to haul him off because of what he and Halland had seen.

They were all skating around things—both the Sleepers and the staff. It was only a matter of time before one side was going to have to make a move. That's all that was left to do. Whomever had brought them all together was waiting to see what that move would be.

Danai tried to see him, but he distanced himself and didn't worry about how it affected her feelings. There were more important matters at hand, and all he wanted to do was think—figure things out. Someone had to. Not that the others weren't trying too. He knew that Oui, Quest, and Tristan were always working on things from a technology standpoint. But somehow, *he* was seen as the leader of the Sleepers. *How did that happen?*

Everyone looked to him for everything. They expected him to know what to do or say next. But he was just like them. Kids trying to find their way—albeit, highly intelligent kids. Why did they act like he was something more?

Aiden stepped into his shower stall. A light mist of water sprayed out of the nozzles that ran down the wall on either side of him. The mist stopped, and the next spray began, mixed with an aloe-based cleanser for sensitive skin.

"Switch to manual," said Aiden. He pressed a dial on the wall and water rained down from a shower head above him. He pressed another dial and the water became warmer, steaming up the stall.

As the water ran down over his head, he leaned forward and placed both hands on the wall in front of him. His head hung low as the water rushed over the back of his head, neck, and back. It felt good. He stayed in that position, inhaled deeply, and exhaled. He couldn't believe what he had just seen. He replayed it all in his mind from beginning to end.

He and Halland had determined what time the floor aide went on break. He'd left his suite and had decided on the stairs rather than the elevator and quickly jogged down.

Aiden had then stopped in front of the door with the AUTHORIZED PERSONNEL ONLY sign flashing above it. His heart sank. There was no way in. The entry had been updated and now required a scan for admittance.

Someone had made sure they would never have access to that wall again. The only way in now would be through his dreams, as Halland had suggested.

Aiden climbed into his chamber. It had to work. He couldn't wait another day. He didn't want to wonder anymore about what was going on. He needed to know what they were facing, the full magnitude of it—to see it firsthand.

He focused his mind on nothing but the vortex energy field until he fell asleep.

In his visionscope, he took the exact steps he'd taken while awake. He left his room and took the stairs rather than the elevator to the first floor, turned left toward the door, and walked right through it to the hallway on the other side.

At the end of the hall, he walked through the vortex energy field and stood looking over the railing at the floors below. People walked past him. He jumped, startled for a moment, having forgotten he was invisible.

First, he went back to the data storage room and stepped in front of one of the glass data partitions that hung from the ceiling. He watched as information scrolled down it, and then looked around at the others in the room. *Interesting.*

It's much busier here at night. He walked around each person, seeing what they were viewing and inputting.

He raised his hand in the air and typed his name on one of the glass screens. *Aiden Quinn. Let's see what they have on me.* His high school I.D. photo appeared. He read quickly as the information scrolled past.

Tech entry: Subject along with Halland Prescott
cracked the code of algorithms during I.Q. test
portion of physical exam.

Aiden watched the footage, unaware he had been filmed when he took the test. He quickly skimmed through the information compiled on him before stopping on a recent file of neuro readings. *How are they getting these readings?*

The file showed that his neuroscans from ten consecutive nights were exactly the same as those of the other nine Sleepers.

"They are almost identical, with minor fluctuations
the first part of the night, as if they have become
one unified brain."

There was footage of a tech laying each Sleeper's brain scan on top of the other to prove they were identical.

"Identical neurological patterns."

He read the transcribed notes of a recorded conversation.

"We need a way to see inside their minds like watching
playback of a recording. It's as if being around each
other has amalgamated them in some way.

"We need to get them under at the same time. I want
to see this in real time. Also, go back over each night's
readings and pinpoint when this began. Match it up to
whatever footage of events you have for that day and
the day before."

They are watching everything we do, thought Aiden.

CHAPTER 51

I n his dream, Aiden left the data storage lab, and in the corridor, watched someone exit a one-man chute. He quickly stepped around him and into the chute, pressing zero for the ground floor.

As the chute lowered past each floor, Aiden looked through the glass and took in everything, hoping he could remember every detail, the workers, labs, and equipment. It was like a whole other technological age down there, more advanced than anything he'd ever seen. As the chute descended, the enclosure went from glass to metal and continued descending after the zero lit up on the panel.

The door opened, and a man stood before him, staring in his direction. Aiden held his breath, his heartbeat quickening. *He can't see you. He can't see you.*

The man turned, lifted his arm toward someone outside, and Aiden slipped past him. He stood a few feet away from the man and watched him. The man turned full circle, looking around himself, and entered the chute looking confused. *He must feel something.*

As the chute door closed, Aiden began breathing again. He looked up and jumped out of the way just before being plowed down by a group of soldiers. His mouth dropped. *This is a military facility.*

Aiden followed the soldiers through the expansive concrete-walled area which resembled a hangar, to a corridor. A woman walked up to a double set of glass doors and scanned her hand, and then her iris. The doors slid open, and he followed her past several labs before she stopped and looked behind her.

Aiden froze in place.

The woman shook her head, turned, and kept walking.

Aiden started to follow her, but looked to his left and spotted a lab. A tech stood blocking his view. He could see feet hanging from a chair in front of the man. The tech stepped to the side, and Aiden approached the glass.

Lax! They're still running tests on him.

Lax looked to be unconscious. Aiden grimaced as he watched a man in a white lab jacket fasten Lax in the chair and inject him with something that made his body violently convulse.

He walked through the glass and over to Lax. This would explain his aggression in the visionscopes. These tests were changing him.

The lab tech took a tube from a centrifuge and added the fluid to a machine. The fluid flowed down through a tube and into another fluid. Aiden followed the tube to see where it would lead. The insertion point was at the base of Lax's skull.

I can't allow this to happen. Aiden wrapped his hands around the tubing and yanked them from the machines, causing the flow to reverse and spill onto the floor.

"What happened? Did you see that?" the man yelled as he backed away from the chair. He watched as equipment all over the lab began to explode. "I thought he was unconscious. Is he making this happen? Hurry, get me another—"

The women in the room screamed as the man's body lifted into the air and slammed into the wall, rendering him unconscious.

What's wrong with you? You could have killed him. Aiden cupped his hands together and watched the shower water puddle into them and run from the tips of his fingers to his wrists, bubbling like a stream.

He thought of the stream from his spring break trip with his mom. As awesome of a memory as it was, none of that mattered anymore. Nothing outside of the Institute mattered. Not when there was a life or lives at stake.

A mixed feeling of anger and hopelessness filled him. Who would ever believe them? Who would come to their rescue?

He splashed water from his hands onto his face and flinched. He felt a sting. His hand flew up and touched his neck as he looked behind him. There was nothing there.

Seconds later, his vision became blurry, and his knees buckled. He fell forward toward the front of the shower. He could no longer think or feel as the shower water sprayed over his torso. The sound of the water running down the drain became distant in his ears as the room began to darken.

CHAPTER 52

Aiden struggled to open his eyes. He groaned, his mouth dry and his head feeling like it had been hit with a sledgehammer. A deep voice echoed in his mind. It was extremely slow and distorted.

"He's awake."

Fire shot across his face. His head darted to the right. *Ow! Did someone just slap me?* His eyes blinked open and shut to blot out the bright lights shining on him.

"Aiden!"

Why is he yelling my name so slowly? Aiden could feel someone moving toward him. He raised his hand as if to say wait. He didn't want to be slapped again. His hand dropped like a lead block back onto his lap.

"Good. We have your attention. Tell us what you know."

"What I know about what?" His voice seemed to be coming from somewhere else. "I don't know anything."

"Sure you do. You've been exploring, haven't you?"

"Everything about my world is fake," he sung with a slurred voice while slumped over the back of the chair. "I'm the only truth in it."

He laughed after the verse and squinted into the light around him while singing the verse again.

"I don't know that song. You're a funny man, Mr. Quinn. Maybe we brought the wrong person here. Maybe we should've brought Danai. That's what we should do."

"Bring her where? Where am I?"

"You're asleep—dreaming in your sleep chamber. As I was saying, I'm sure we could get Danai—no, Farmer—to answer our questions. Does she know something?"

Aiden's head turned toward the sound of the squeal of a chair being dragged toward him. "No, leave her out of it," he replied as his head dropped. "Get Brooks," he grumbled. "She's one of you any way. Do what you want to her." He attempted to laugh at the last part, but all that came out was a heavy puff of air.

All was silent for a moment.

The voice was closer to him now. "Tell us about Farmer. What does she know, Mr. Quinn?"

"She knows everything."

A woman's voice met his ears. "The scan shows he's telling the truth."

The man continued, "Really? What does she know?"

"She knows what I know."

"And what would that be, Mr. Quinn?"

Pain seared behind his eyes, more intense than any migraine he'd ever had. He groaned as he raised his hands and held the sides of his head.

"Is that supposed to be happening?" someone asked.

"I don't know," another voice replied.

The man repeated his question. "What do you know, Mr. Quinn?"

A voice echoed in his head. *"Aiden. Wake up."* It was his voice, but it wasn't him speaking to himself. *"Wake up!"*

"I know . . ." Aiden's eyes rolled back. "I know that I need to wake up," he said clearly as he began to sit up.

Aiden heard bodies moving quickly around him as he became more aware.

"It's not possible. He's bringing himself out. Hurry, inject him again."

Aiden attempted to stand as someone grabbed each of his arms and pushed him back down. He tried fighting them, but more hands grabbed him. They were rough and heavy, applying too much weight for him to bear. He flinched, feeling the bee sting again.

Aiden's eyes blinked open. *Am I drowning?* He coughed, choking on the water on the floor of his shower and slowly pulled himself up. *Did I pass out? Was I dreaming?*

CHAPTER 53

MRS. QUINN

M rs. Quinn boarded a redline Teslaloop bound for the northeast quadrant of the city. There, she followed several confusing signs to a private rail that traveled directly to Carnival, where she would meet Coulter.

She feared she would regret the visit as soon as she saw the entrance approaching ahead.

The rail shot through a dark tunnel, a trick to heighten your senses as it exited into an explosion of bright, colorful lights and music.

Mrs. Quinn exited the vessel faster than she wanted to, being pushed forward by the excited passengers. Their eyes darted in every direction.

Carnival, a major tourist attraction, was an amusement park of sorts. A nightly festival with live music and street dancing with people wearing a sundry of costumes.

A kaleidoscope of color surrounded her and continued up five stories into the sky. She ducked past a float and out of the way of a parade. There were various forms of parades on different levels, some to be watched by the public, while others were meant for public participation. If caught passing by, you could easily be pulled into the parade as everyone in the vicinity was made to dance.

Mrs. Quinn walked through the amusement park rides and V-R gaming centers toward the extreme restaurants. She stopped at a virtual menu sign, seeing a burger the size of a person's head with a side of fried tarantulas. Overhead, a woman screamed with laughter, her feet dangling high above the crowd via cables that carried her seating over the park while she dined.

"I guess that's why they call them extreme restaurants."

A water slide climbed around structures and dropped three stories to a glass bottom pool suspended in the air over visitors. It was all quite a spectacle, and for some like her, a little overwhelming.

Coulter stood atop a balcony filled with partying park goers and climbed down the metal trellis next to it. "Mrs. Quinn," he called as he waved.

She waved back and kept her arm raised as she pushed past a couple of half-dressed human flamingos. She could spot Coulter anywhere. Pretty much the same height and size as Aiden, mocha skin, a head full of tiny dark curls, shorter on the sides and higher on the top—the only haircut he'd ever had. Except now, the sides were even lower and tapered off to a V at his neck, and the top was higher.

"Coulter, hey." She hugged him, noticing the appearance of a faint mustache and deciding against teasing him about it. "This is quite a place."

"First time here?"

She looked around and nodded while a woman wearing a white bodysuit sauntered through the crowd. Her costume included a set of wings that spread out almost the width of a skywalk. "Yep, first and last," she replied.

He laughed and took her by the arm. "There is a reason I asked you here . . ."

They stepped onto a travelator that glided until it became an escalator, moving them up to the next level of the park. Mrs. Quinn looked down and all around them. As they climbed, fireworks spread across the sky.

She glanced at Coulter, noticing his mouth moving, and held a finger in one ear. "I couldn't hear you. What did you say?"

"This way!" he yelled.

The entrance to the cinema was on the far side of an outdoor restaurant. Patrons placed orders on holo-screens and watched the fireworks as trays rose from the tables, adorned with colorful drinks.

There were just as many people on that level as the previous one. Mrs. Quinn feared they would get separated, but then Coulter grabbed her arm again and handed her something. *Is it a tracker in case he loses me?* She glanced at the object and held it tightly in her hand as he continued to pull her forward.

Various people in the crowd bumped into him. She noticed he handed each of them a similar object, at least eight people who fanned out in opposite directions.

They approached the cinema, and Coulter placed his hand on the scanner to show he had already purchased tickets. A washable barcode appeared on his wrist, and then on Mrs. Quinn's.

Coulter released her arm as they entered the cinema, leading the way into the theatre. They sat at the back in a pair of fluffy red recliner seats that adjusted to their weight and height and swiveled in any direction. A table sat between them for food. Mrs. Quinn looked around. "There's no one here."

He smiled. "I know."

She pointed her index finger at him and wiggled it up and down. "*You . . .*" She looked down at the object she was still holding, flipped it over, and held it up. "What is this?"

"Let's see, how can I put this in terms you would understand?"

"Try me."

"There's an invisible barrier around us that no one can get through. No cameras, radar, audio devices—nothing gets through. That's why each person I handed one to fanned out in a circle around us. Right here in this theatre, we are at the center of the barrier and undetectable."

"A dead zone. I thought it was a tracker."

"I wouldn't need a gadget to track you."

She was impressed, but why would he go to such lengths just to take her to the movies? "What do you know?"

"Too much to say. Put this on."

"Eyewear?"

"Not exactly."

She looked at the thin square-lensed glasses as if she wasn't sure she should put them on, then carefully placed the lenses over her eyes.

Coulter watched her while tapping his fingers over his wristband.

"Oh, crap!" Mrs. Quinn yelled as information began to scroll down the lenses in green. She snatched the glasses off and rubbed her eyes. "Could you not have warned me?" She put the glasses back on, but not as close to her eyes as before.

"Talk to it."

"Excuse me?"

"Tell the lenses exactly what you need them to do."

Mrs. Quinn spoke aloud. "Slow down." She smiled as she watched. "Decrease font. Expand."

When Mrs. Quinn finally took the glasses off, she squeezed the area between her eyes and blinked hard. "I have so many questions right now. Where do I start?" Her eyes adjusted, and she saw there was pizza, French fries, and sodas on the table.

"You know me too well." She grabbed a plate and a slice of pizza. "The key is to take a bite of pizza first and chew it a little, and then add a couple of French fries to your mouth like so," she said with her mouth full. "Try it."

Coulter copied her with his veggie, non-dairy slice and smiled. "It's good. I've never thought about that combination."

It was only a personal sized pizza, but Mrs. Quinn's was gone in no time. She looked up as she wiped sauce from her lip, noticing Coulter's expression. "I'm a bit of a nervous eater. I'll eat anything in sight and pay for it later with an upset stomach."

"You're fun, cooler than most parents. I can see why you and Aiden are so close."

"Thank you, Coulter. That's very kind of you to say."

He became solemn. "Why wouldn't Aiden tell his best friend he was a Sleeper?"

Mrs. Quinn looked up from her drink at Coulter's downcast eyes. "I'm sure it wasn't personal. We kept it from everyone. I think he wanted your relationship to remain the same. You made him feel normal. He loves you, you know. Though he may never use those words to tell you. You're like a brother to him. I don't think he wanted to chance losing that. He probably feared you would see him as some type of freak if you knew."

"I wouldn't have. You didn't."

"But I'm his mother. It's different. It's been hard, and I suppose too much for a normal person to handle. But that's my baby, my heart," she said while placing her fist on her chest.

She set her cup down. Her eyes teared. It was the first time since finding out there was something going on at the Institute that she allowed herself to let go. She sniffed and wiped her eye. "Your research is thorough, most of which I've seen."

"What's keeping him at the institute? Why won't he leave?"

"He's not the only one. There are other Sleepers there. You know him. He won't leave his friends behind. At this point, I'm not sure he even can. You yourself know that someone is following and watching us."

"Yeah, they tried to hack into my system."

"Really?" Mrs. Quinn smiled. "They didn't know who they were dealing with."

"Exactly. Is there someone on the inside maybe who could help?"

"We have someone. One of the teachers. She posts codes to me through the school media network. The last one stated to check out Professor Houser."

Coulter made note of it on his wrist band. "Tell her to stop doing that. Secret codes—the kind you learn about in school?" He shook his head. "Much too easy to decipher."

"I thought the same thing."

"Aiden has a CPU wallet I made for him."

"Yes, I sent it to him through her."

"She needs to let him know about anything of importance, and he can get it to us—you—so we can work on getting him home."

Listen to him trying to sound grown and in charge.

Coulter held up a finger, and the movie began.

"What are you doing?"

"We came to watch a movie, didn't we?"

"What is it?"

"Jalousie Island."

"It had better not be anything creepy."

"Relax, Mom," Coulter responded with a grin.

COULTER

INTERCEPTED TRANSMISSION SENT TO COULTER'S WRIST-BAND.

Coulter noticed the blinking light and tapped his wristband to listen. A voice he didn't recognize came through the speakers.

"Sir, I don't know what they are using, but we can't see or hear them."

Another voice came through. "You have the technology to see through walls."

"Nothing, sir. We can't get any audio or visual."

"You've got to be kidding me. Send a unit in." He hesitated. "In plain clothes. Make sure they are not harmed."

"Sir, they're inside watching a film."

"They may be, but they are not jamming our signal just to watch a film, and where would civilians get the technology to do this?"

"Should we move in?"

"That should be obvious. Move in."

Coulter sat up in his seat and read the message that followed.

They're coming. Use back exit.

"Mrs. Quinn, we have to go." Coulter stood and walked past the rows of seats toward the screen. Mrs. Quinn followed him through a dark passage behind it to a door, then down a dark hallway to another door. Coulter typed into his wristband.

At back exit.

A second later he received a response. *Wait.*

He turned to Mrs. Quinn. "Take your jacket off."

She watched him as he turned his plaid shirt inside out, revealing a tan interior.

His wristband blinked with another message. *What color is she wearing?*

White, he typed back.

"You kids really thought this out. I'm impressed," Mrs. Quinin said.

"Be impressed after we get us out of here."

"Do they know Aiden?"

"No, they know me, and they care what happens to me, just like I care what happens to Aiden."

"I don't think the world knows what kind of minds you kids have."

"Someone knows. That's why they want us. That's why they want Aiden."

He watched his wrist for a few seconds. *Now!* it responded.

Coulter quickly opened the door and dashed out, grabbing Mrs. Quinn by the arm. They ducked down as they maneuvered through a group of intoxicated Carnival attendees.

Special-ops soldiers headed them off near the plaza of street artists in body paint posing as statues. They grabbed at them, but each time found it was someone else. They were Coulter's friends, dressed in the exact same tan shirt and a girl with a white top.

"We have to get underground."

"No, back to my place. Come on," said Mrs. Quinn.

"Why?"

"They can't touch us there."

CHAPTER 54

MRS. QUINN

Mrs. Quinn led Coulter into her home. "Black out," she told the home assistant bot. All the preset lighting for when she entered at night turned off, leaving the space as dark as a cave. "When they don't find us at the park, they will look for us here."

"Do you think the government is involved? Those were soldiers."

"Organizations hire soldiers after their tour is over, so it's hard to say. This way." She walked back toward Coulter and grabbed his arm, realizing he couldn't make his way through in the dark, and took him to her office. "Seal it," she said aloud. A steel door slid shut behind them. "Lights." Nothing happened.

"They must already know we're here and have switched the power off," said Coulter.

"Doesn't matter. My assistant, as well as everything in this room, runs on another power source. The walls are reinforced with steel plates. I had this place special designed. The architect couldn't make sense of it. Tab, alternate power." She pushed buttons in the air, and the room lit up.

"Wow."

"You haven't seen anything yet. I have a secret security system Aiden didn't know about. If he had, he could dream about it and alter it."

A virtual controller appeared in front of her.

"You could possibly be the coolest mom that ever lived."

"Of course, I am. Get ready."

On the display wall, they watched green figures enter the home and separate to search different areas. One soldier motioned for part of their team to head upstairs.

"How can they see?" Counter asked.

"They're wearing night vision gear and are seeing things the same way we are seeing them right now."

Mrs. Quinn tapped her fingers in the air and footage of several areas around the building appeared. Soldiers were climbing up the stairwell, while others in plain clothes attempted to appear as residents on the three lobby levels of the high rise. The footage also showed an empty roof.

"Just about there," she said slowly as soldiers moved down the hall. Her hand pushed forward over the controller, and steel walls slammed across the hall, sealing off soldiers in the separate areas where they stood. They banged on the walls and tried to kick through them to no avail.

"Bad move, guys." She pushed a button. A trap floor released and closed behind them, sealing them below.

"Where does that lead?"

"I'm not quite sure. Maybe the incinerator?"

Coulter looked shocked and shook his head.

Mrs. Quinn held out her hands. "Quick, choose your weapon. Taser or stun gun?"

"Aren't they the same thing?"

"No, and it bothers me that you don't know that."

"Do we really need those?"

Mrs. Quinn stared at him.

"Okay, whatever. Stun gun. What now?"

"To the roof."

The home assistant bot's voice cut through the air. "Goodbye, Mrs. Quinn. It was a pleasure serving you."

"Why is your bot saying that—like this is the end or something?"

"Don't worry about that. Tab, you have thirty seconds. Upload yourself into my wristband until I can get you to your new home."

"Thank you, Mrs. Quinn."

Her wristband lit up, and she pointed at the corner of the office where the wall panel slid back and revealed a one-man chute.

"We can't both fit in there."

"We're going to have to," she said as she lifted a crossbody bag over her head and entered the chute.

Coulter stared at the tight enclosure.

She knew he was trying to figure out how he would fit in. If he faced her, he would press up against her breasts. If he turned away from her, she would press against his backside. Neither option was appropriate.

Hearing the first of several explosions made him jump into the chute—face to face.

Mrs. Quinn pressed a button, wrapped her arms around him, and they jetted to the roof.

Awkward!

The one-man chute opened inside a shed on the roof that was locked from the inside. With a scan of Mrs. Quinn's iris, the door slid open. Coulter stepped out onto the roof and stared at an aircraft. Mrs. Quinn ran to it and removed the clips that connected to bolts on the floor.

"Whoa, is that yours?" he asked.

"I pay for the parking spot."

"Are you a secret agent?"

"Nope, just prepared."

"Prepared for what? Why do you have all of this?"

"My line of work. The kind of people I take to trial often make death threats, and I have a son to protect. Not only that, I have a Sleeper for a son."

"I—I'm not getting in there. Do you even have a license?"

"Of course, I do," she said with a smirk.

"There has to be someone that can help us. We can go to the police or the FBI."

The engine of the craft began to whir.

Sheesh, kid! What happened to the confident genius I was just with at Carnival? I guess this is out of his comfort zone.

"I know you're smarter than that, Coulter. You're scared, so you're not thinking straight." She jumped into the front seat and placed her palm on a control that caused the engine to rev louder. She motioned for him to get in. "I need you to think like an adult right now. We're talking government agencies here. That is a government agency that has Aiden. There is no one."

She reached over and forcibly pulled him into the seat. "Buckle up."

"Ouch. That hurt."

¡*Gallina!* "Hold on, Coulter!" She yelled as she watched soldiers swarm the roof, shooting at the aircraft.

CHAPTER 55

COULTER

C oulter hurried and fastened his harness. He braced himself as the vehicle lurched forward, slamming his head back against the headrest. He held tight to the armrest as the vehicle approached the edge of the roof. Only, the aircraft didn't lift off.

They flipped over the side of the building and kept descending as Coulter screamed, with one hand on the roof of the craft and the other out to his right on the window.

They cut through smoke, fog, and various levels of the city before Coulter looked around Mrs. Quinn's seat and saw they were approaching the ground. But they weren't stopping.

Coulter screamed even louder, seeing they were going to slam into the top of a shipping container.

Just before impact, the top of the container slid back and opened to a passage, and another opened beneath it, admitting them below ground.

Coulter looked behind them as he continued screaming. They had been on a track the entire time. The track receded back into the wall and disappeared. The passage to the rail quickly sealed off, and they continued through it like a tram.

He looked down. "Why are we on a bridge underground? What's below us?" He yelled out between screams.

The vehicle began to reduce speed and came to a stop next to a platform.

"You can stop screaming now," yelled Mrs. Quinn.

Coulter quieted himself and caught his breath. "Are—are you Batman?" he asked, shaking while climbing out.

A man stood on the platform before steel doors. He walked forward. "Your module alerted me of an emergency departure. Per your very detailed protocol, I'm here to take you to a safe house."

"Jaxxon to the rescue." Mrs. Quinn smiled. "Did you arrange security?"

"Of course."

She looked past Jaxxon. "Hey Coulter, meet my friend, Jaxxon."

"Jaxxon? As in Jaxxon with two x's?"

Mrs. Quinn looked confused. "Yes. How did you know that?"

Coulter quickly stepped toward the man with a smile, shoved the stun gun to his abdomen, and zapped him.

"What are you doing?" Mrs. Quinn yelled as Jaxxon fell to the ground, shaking.

"He's the reason I contacted you to meet up. It was just bad timing on his part that I happened upon him retrieving information. They know everything about you."

"Who? He's hired by many."

"Wherever you thought he was going to take you, he had been instructed to by whomever is running the Institute. Mrs. Quinn, I know I'm just a kid. You don't have to believe me, but I care about you like you were my own mom, and if I thought you were in danger—"

Two prongs shot out of Mrs. Quinn's taser and grabbed onto Jaxxon's back. He yelled out as his muscles contracted and his body shook.

"There's duct tape in my bag. Grab it," instructed Mrs. Quinn.

"What are you doing?"

"Checking him for a map."

"He's got a pistol."

"I'll take that," she said and placed it in her waist band. "He was supposed to get me the layout of an old naval facility. That's where I need to go."

"Let me do it." Coulter ran a scanner over him from his wristband. "Got it." He studied the image. "Aiden did research on this."

Mrs. Quinn looked up, surprised. "On what?"

"What was beneath the city. It was for a history paper. We talked about the quadrant transit rail, but this isn't it. What is this place?"

"It doesn't exist. At least not for the majority of society."

"But *you* know about it."

"I'm privileged."

"What does that mean?"

"I have the security clearance."

"Security clearance? Wait, so that means this is government, and since you know about this, you must have the highest level of clearance," he said almost to himself. "You being an attorney is not enough to get you this type of clearance. You're not who everyone thinks you are, are you? What do you really do?"

"There he is. He's back," Mrs. Quinn joked. "This rail line is the most discreet way to transport the most powerful man in the world."

"The President?" Coulter exclaimed, his eyes wide.

"And his family, press, officials, and secret service agents."

Coulter looked over at the man who was now bound in duct tape. "He's secret service?"

"Former."

Mrs. Quinn studied the hologram image of a rail system. "Look. This rail connects to this one." She enlarged the naval facility layout. "Whatever is under that facility has a tunnel attached."

"That's where Aiden is?"

"That's my way into where Aiden is."

"What do you mean *your* way in? I'm going with you."

"Coulter, I can't take any further chances with your safety."

"I'm not letting you go alone."

"Your parents would have a fit—"

"They probably already have my parents."

"Coulter, I can't—"

"¡*Basta Ya*!" Coulter exclaimed.

"Don't tell me to stop it. You stop it. If your parents have been taken, then that means you are now my responsibility. Therefore, I have to keep you safe, which I have done a good job of so far, I might add."

Coulter thought for a moment. "Unless you're going to lock me up somewhere, the only way to keep me safe would be to take me with you. Who knows what I will get into by myself," he stated with a sly grin.

"I swear, you and Aiden. Sheesh, get in."

"You mean, you can actually drive this thing? I thought it worked by some form of slingshot propulsion. Just to be clear, we don't have to drop down again, right?"

TRANSMISSION

"Sir, we've lost the woman and the boy."

"Where are they?"

"They dove off the building."

"They're dead?"

"We don't know. Images are coming in from the ground level right now. Nothing but shipping houses, sir."

He spoke of rectangular metal boxes that were formerly shipping containers. It was the housing of choice for the indigent citizens and the lower levelers that lived on the ground level of the city—the place that upper levelers rarely saw or visited.

"Call the teams in. Put out an all-points bulletin with the MPD."

"Are we discrediting her—saying she's kidnapped the kid?"

"No, not yet. First things first. Find them before this gets any further out of hand."

CHAPTER 56

Aiden opened his eyes. An orange-red wave flowed over him. He jumped and rubbed his eyes. Someone watched him through the glass cover of his chamber—a girl with long red hair. He blinked, and she was gone.

He pressed the release for his chamber to open, sat up, and looked around. The room was empty. *I'm seeing things.*

How did I even get into my chamber? The last thing he remembered was laying on the floor of his shower.

He hopped over the side of the chamber, ran to the bathroom, and stood over the sink, staring at himself. He grimaced. *Man, my head hurts.* Had it all been a dream, or was someone trying to make him believe it was?

The day's schedule scrolled down the left side of his mirror. His eyes widened. *What time is it?*

He squinted at the tiny numbers flashing in red on the bottom of the mirror. He had already missed two classes. He dressed hurriedly and dashed out of the dorm to find his friends before they entered their next class.

As Aiden jogged past the courtyard, a guy he'd never seen before reached for his shoulder. "Hey, Aiden." Aiden moved out of his grasp and kept going.

"Aiden!" a female voice called out moments later.

He turned and saw Brooks waving at him.

She jogged up to him. "Hey, did you know Lax is looking for you?"

"Is he?"

"Yes. What's wrong? Are you okay?"

"I'm fine."

"Aiden, wait. Stop." She placed her hand on his arm and lightly pulled.

He started to pull out of her reach like he did the last guy. Instead, he stopped and looked up at the sky. *Here we go.*

"I know you don't like me," she said. "But I don't know what to do about it. I don't know what I've done to turn you against me. If you're worried about Lax, I'm not going to hurt him. I care deeply about him. I'm not the enemy."

Aiden leaned forward into Brooks's face and turned toward her ear. "I saw you," he whispered and backed away.

She looked confused. "What do you mean, 'you saw me?' What did you see?"

Aiden turned.

"Don't walk away from me, Aiden."

He stopped again. "You were in that lab, screaming as the equipment blew up around the room. You were there while they ran experiments on the guy you just said you care so much about. Deeply, right? That's what you said? Yeah, I saw you."

Brooks slowly backed up as he stepped closer to her.

"Test Subject Alpha Ten. You helped with the serum. You probably even injected him. How did you feel when he convulsed? Did you forget how deeply you cared during those tests?"

"Aiden . . ."

"What? What the hell could you possibly have to say to me?"

Brooks froze. "If they can't control you, they're not going to let you live."

Aiden backed away from her. There it was. Those few words revealed that everything he'd thought about her and the Institute was true. There was no way they could stay any longer. He couldn't explain why he awoke crawling out of his shower, but he was least concerned about himself. He would make sure that was the last time the institute would ever experiment on Lax.

Aiden frantically searched the campus for Lax. He finally ran into him leaving an Anatomy and Physiology lecture, heading to his next class.

"A, where have you been? You missed test prep and the last view of the cadaver in lab," said Lax.

"I guess I was really tired. I must have slept right through the alarm. Did you dream last night?"

"Why are you asking that? You know what? I don't remember dreaming at all."

"I really need to talk to you. Can we go—"

"I can't afford to miss test prep for semester finals. Remember? Nothing less than ninety percent? Why do you look so crazed? Come on. We can talk about whatever it is on the way to class." He wrapped his arm around Aiden's shoulders. "Your boy is here for you. What did she do? Is she cheating?"

Aiden noticed something was off about Lax in their next class.

"A, why are you watching me?"

"Are you okay?" asked Aiden.

Lax frowned. "My head is throbbing. I can't get my thoughts together."

A few minutes later, Lax zoned out. Aiden waved a hand in front of his face. It was as if he wasn't even there. *What have they done to you?*

"We're getting out of here," said Aiden.

"What was that, Mr. Quinn? Did you have something to share on the structure of nucleic acids?" the professor asked.

Aiden shook his head and stood. "No, sir. I'm just tired of all of this and what you've done to my friend." He looked at Lax.

Lax jerked to attention, then pointed at himself. "To who? Me? He hasn't done anything to me."

"Get up," said Aiden. "Let's go."

The other Sleepers in the class, uncertain of what was going on, what exactly Aiden meant, or what he was going to do, slowly began to rise also.

My mom was right about this place from the beginning, Aiden thought as he walked toward the door. Lax didn't move.

The professor crossed his arms. "Mr. Quinn, I suggest you and your friends get back in your seats. The lecture is almost over."

"It's already over for us," Aiden replied.

At the front of the class, a muscular, bowlegged student with a crew cut rose from his seat and turned to face Aiden, blocking off his exit. Aiden stepped to the side and the student moved in front of him as if he were teaching Aiden how to ballroom dance.

Aiden looked up at him. His facial expression was unreadable, but his eyes were threatening, and his shoulders tight and raised.

Aiden focused on the pounding pulse in his neck. *I'm over it.*

"The charade is over," Aiden sneered. "Let's be real. Clearly, you are a grown man and not a teenager."

The guy looked over at the professor, who nodded at him. He grabbed Aiden. Aiden struggled to twist out of his grasp. The man's taut muscles wrapped around Aiden's neck and choked him. Aiden's arms swung wildly, reaching up behind him to grab hold of some part of the man's face.

He was unable to break free from his grip, and he turned red as he tried his best to breathe. His eyes began to roll back.

"He's going to kill him," yelled Danai.

Tristan, Fitz, and Bale ran forward.

"Don't do it," the man stated. "I'll snap his neck."

"No, you won't. You need him," said Tristan.

Danai turned and screamed. "Lax! Lax!"

Lax, still seated, looked ahead with a dazed expression, as if he wasn't even seeing what was going on. Danai ran to him and shook him while still calling his name. His eyes began to focus, as if he had just been released from some internal prison and was free to see the world.

Lax dashed to the front of the class. The man leaned back, lifting Aiden off the floor, and took quick steps, falling back into the display wall behind him.

"Bad move," said Lax.

His speed was what won his high school football games. He ran forward and kicked the guy's right foot out from under him, causing him to fall to the side, landing on his knee, his other leg still extended.

The man didn't make a sound, but the twisted expression on his face was enough to let Lax know he'd hurt him. He moved swiftly, stepping his foot inside of the attacker's. With his adrenaline pumping, he flipped both Aiden and the attacker over onto the floor. His fist slammed into the attacker's face, and Tristan and Bale pulled Aiden away.

Aiden leaned over a desk, gasping for air with Danai at his side. She brushed his hair away from his face.

Students were standing all over the room, but they didn't move.

Tristan and Bale stepped in front of the Professor with a stance that dared him to make a move.

"Let's go," Fitz said as he assisted Aiden in standing.

"You won't get far." The professor smirked before receiving a blow to the face from Tristan.

The professor didn't flinch. He smiled at them, the smile of an evil genius. He began to glow, as did the eight other students in the room that stood at attention, watching them.

"What is happening?" Danai nervously whispered as they backed toward the door.

"Stop them!" the professor yelled.

On the display wall of the classroom, words appeared.

SUBJECTS ON THE RUN

Lax and Fitz helped Aiden as they ran out of the room. It was apparent the words had appeared on the display wall of all the classes. The door of each classroom slid open, and students poured out of the lecture halls after them.

"In here," said Danai, pointing at a room at the end of the hall. "There's another exit."

They followed her inside, and the door slid shut behind them.

Aiden stood hunched over, holding his neck.

"What is going on? I thought they were students like us," said Fitz.

"No one is like us," Bale replied.

"Evidently, they—all of them—work for whoever's trying to keep us here," said Tristan.

"But they were glowing, and I'm not so sure I want to stay here and find out why. What are we doing?" asked Fitz, looking around the room.

Danai pointed to a door down the steps on the opposite side of the lecture hall. "We're going there. Down there."

"You okay, man?" asked Lax.

Aiden nodded and waved his hand for them to keep going.

"What's outside that door?"

"The larger lecture halls have a back door that the professors and their assistants use to enter and exit. It leads to a private hallway."

"Go," Aiden said.

They all ran toward the exit at the far end of the room. Just as Aiden reached it, the door slid shut, locking him and Danai inside the room.

CHAPTER 57

Tristan and Bale yelled out to Aiden and Danai while banging and kicking at the door. Aiden and Danai pounded on the other side.

Fitz searched the wall for a mechanism to release the lock but found none.

Lax stepped in front of the door. "There's no way in there. We have to keep going." He grabbed Tristan and Bale and pushed them toward the hall.

"We're just going to leave them?"

"They'll find us, and if they don't—" He tapped the side of his head. "We'll find them. Go. We can't wait."

"Aiden wouldn't have left us," Tristan stated as they approached the end of the hall.

"Do I look like Aiden to you? If you want to go back, go back. No one is forcing you."

Tristan and Bale exchanged glances. They hesitated, then continued on.

Their pace slowed, and they tried to act normal while passing several offices on either side of the corridor.

At the end of the hall, they turned right. "Wait a minute," Bale whispered as he squatted low against the wall and peeked around the corner.

"What do you see?" asked Fitz.

Bale swung his arm at him for him to shut up. He stood and leaned back against the wall. "Right around this corner is the door to the outside, but those crazy students are at the far end of the hall that separates us from the door. It's only about six steps to get past that opening. There are stairs on the left, but I'm sure security is on them."

They looked back and forth at each other. "We don't have much of a choice here. Do we walk or crawl?" asked Fitz.

"Whatever we do, we need to hurry before they head down this way," said Tristan.

Before anyone could respond, he stepped out into the corridor just as cracks of gunfire from what sounded like a semi-automatic weapon came from the other side of the building. Tristan jumped back, and they all ducked.

Bale peeked around the corner again. "They're running toward the gunfire."

"Go," said Lax, pushing them forward.

Once they crossed the corridor, Lax peeked back around the corner while Tristan and Bale investigated the stairwell. Fitz aggressively pounded on Lax's arm, as if he were chopping on a chopping board.

"What?" Lax turned to see four students step in front of the exit double doors.

"Go back," the students said in unison.

Tristan and Bale ran down the stairs and stood behind Lax and Fitz.

"What is this, now?" asked Tristan. "The door was clear."

"There's four of us and four of them," said Bale. "If we're getting out of here, it's through those doors." He looked at Lax.

"I don't know," said Fitz. "They don't look right. Their eyes are kind of glazed over."

"Let's do it." Lax gave the nod, and they stepped toward the students blocking their exit.

Click.

They stopped walking.

Click, click. The sound correlated with the student's movements.

"What are they doing?" asked Bale.

The students' arms connected and locked together, becoming one unit, and attached to the door, barricading it. A blue light emitted where their arms fused.

"Whoa, whoa, whoa! What the heck is that?" yelled Fitz. His legs moved like he wanted to run, but he didn't know in what direction.

"They're not real. They're sims, like the orientation leaders that first day," said Lax.

The four students spoke with one voice. "Go back to class."

Fitz took a step back and tripped into Professor Houser, who had come up behind them. "I heard the gunfire. I can get you out. This way," he said, heading down the hall. "Follow me. Hurry."

Fitz turned to follow him, but Lax grabbed his arm. "Don't trust him. They're all in it together."

Fitz looked back, but Professor Houser was gone.

From the second level, Oui and Quest ran down the stairs toward them. Oui's face was bruised and red on the right side.

"What happened?" asked Tristan.

"A couple of the students grabbed him. Don't worry. The other guy looks worse. I made sure of it," said Quest. He and Tristan bumped fists.

"Why are you guys even out of class?" asked Lax.

"You mean you didn't hear the announcement?"

"What announcement?"

"'This is not a drill.' They didn't realize we would see 'Subjects on the run' flashing red on the display wall. I looked at Oui, and we figured it was you and that it was time to go."

"Where's Hal?"

"He was right behind us," said Oui, turning around.

"Please tell me he didn't go to the SkyTran," Tristan responded. "They'll trap him in there."

"Where's Aiden?"

"He and Danai are locked in a lecture hall."

"Where?" asked Oui.

They turned back to see students walking toward them, blocking them off from getting to their friends.

CHAPTER 58

anai sat on the floor of the lecture hall and half laughed with tears in her eyes. "Maybe if we went to sleep, we could get out of here."

Aiden knelt in front of her and clasped her hands in his. "It's going to be okay. We're going to get out of here."

"What do they want from us? Why won't they freaking let us go?"

She's losing it, thought Aiden. He let go of her hands and leaned in, bringing his face close to hers. He placed the palm of his hand on the side of her face. Warm tears ran down her cheek and over his fingers. He looked into her eyes. "I'm not going to let anything happen to you, okay?"

Danai nodded. Her eyes looked away from him as her head tilted slightly. "What's that?"

Aiden looked behind him. Smoke billowed into the room. *Oh, no!* "Come on." They ran to the back door, pulling their shirts up over their noses and mouths.

Danai banged on the door as Aiden looked around.

"Aiden, what are you doing?"

"If we can't get through the door, maybe we can get through the wall."

Danai began to cough. "My eyes are burning."

Aiden picked up a chair. "Move back."

He rammed the chair into the display wall. Small cracks expanded out from the impact. *This is going to take too long. There has to be a quicker way.*

"Danai!" Aiden dropped the chair and ran over to her as she fell to her knees.

The back entrance slid open. He sprung up and jumped in front of Danai to protect her from whoever was entering.

A familiar male voice came from the entrance. "Hurry, follow the second door all the way through and out the back."

Aiden hesitated and looked back at Danai.

"Son, you have no time to think about it. Get her up. Go!"

CHAPTER 59

"Nice," said Oui while approaching the bots barricading the door. He began typing in the air on the virtual keyboard projecting from his wristband.

"What are you doing?" Lax asked.

Quest smiled and watched, knowing the program they'd created was meant for such a time as this.

"Ripping through their structure and overriding their mainframes." He tapped on his arm once. "Done."

A fizzle of sparks exploded in front of them, and the sims were gone.

"Come on," Lax yelled, and they ran outside.

He stopped running when he reached the center of the quad. "Wait, no one's following us. Why isn't anyone following us?"

"Look!" yelled Fitz.

Aiden and Danai ran toward them from the side of the building.

"How did you get out?" Lax asked them.

"Houser," Aiden replied.

"Professor Houser?"

"Yeah, I know."

"We need to get out of here," said Fitz.

"Not without everyone. Who's missing?" Aiden looked around. "Where's Hal?"

"He's on the SkyTran heading for the dorm," said Fitz.

"I think Farmer is in her room," said Danai.

"Come on!" Aiden shouted.

They sprinted toward the dorm. Aiden couldn't believe what he was seeing as they approached the SkyTran. "Look!"

CHAPTER 60

MRS. QUINN

Coulter held a hand over his nose and mouth and shone a light at the walls and up at the rounded ceiling. "I thought the rail would end at a tunnel." He backed up toward the tram. "This is a sewer."

"Well, Coulter," Mrs. Quinn began as she climbed out of the tram. "How can I say this in terms you would understand," she said, mimicking him. "To build that transmitter you used to black us out at Carnival, calculations were involved regarding recovery algorithms, location, and target. If the trajectory turned out to be wrong, there's nothing to do but recalculate and correct it, right?"

"How did you know that?"

"You would be surprised at what I know."

"Uh, no, I wouldn't. So what you're trying to say is we're going to have to figure it out from here. Got it. Actually . . ." Coulter paused while viewing the layout diagram. "We should be directly under or next to what's under the facility. Which way should we go?"

Mrs. Quinn took a flash pointer from her bag and shone it at the ground. They looked down at the water flowing past their feet. "That way, the direction it's flowing from."

The more they walked, the more overbearing the stench in the tunnel became. "I'll never be able to eat again," Coulter stated. "What a day we've had."

"You have no idea what time it is, do you? It's morning, we've been walking a long time."

"Morning? Like the next day? My mom is going to kill me."

Mrs. Quinn stopped walking and held out her arm, stopping Coulter from moving forward. "Listen. Do you hear that?"

Coulter nodded.

A continuous low hum came from above. She took slow steps while shining her pen light across the wall. "There," she said as she pointed.

They stepped up onto a ledge. "I'll go first, so I can protect you from whatever is up there."

"Yeah, right, Coulter. You're just in a hurry to get out of this tunnel." Mrs. Quinn followed him up the makeshift ladder to a passage that led to a transit tunnel.

"Where to now?" Coulter asked.

"You really think I have all the answers, don't you?"

"Well, I have an answer. The computer wallet I made for Aiden has a form of GPS tracker, and we may be close enough to pick up its signal. However, I don't know how well it works from underground."

Mrs. Quinn began to smile.

CHAPTER 61

FARMER

"You've got this, Farm," she told herself as she looked at her reflection in the bathroom mirror. "Now, you go and ace this exam." A smile spread over her face as she slipped her arms into her jacket and pulled her sleeves over her bracelets.

She had chosen to miss class to get in some last-minute studying before her exam. *What is that?* There was ringing in her ears, mixed with other sounds. She closed her eyes and focused on what she was hearing. She needed to separate the sounds. Yelling, Aiden's voice, voices over radios, feet running over pavement. *How am I able to hear all of this?*

From the corner of her eye, she saw movement and looked out of her window. Aiden and the other Sleepers raced across the courtyard toward the dorm. *What's going on?* They were waving their arms and yelling up at the SkyTran. She looked up and to the side, where she could see a portion of the SkyTran rail. Men were out on top of the rail, cautiously making their way to the capsule that hung below it.

Glass shattered and fell from the capsule. Someone began to climb out. *Who is that? No. What is he doing? Did it stop working?*

Halland slipped and pulled himself back up, struggling to climb on top of the rail.

Farmer ran for her gym bag and clamped her team airball risers under her shoes. Just as she fixed the last strap over the top of her laces, a panel on the wall across from her chamber cracked, hissed, and opened. She jumped back, seeing a man emerge. *Aiden said they had a way of getting into our rooms.* She worked her hand behind her, searching for the latch to open the window. *Hurry, hurry, hurry.* Her hand found the knob. *Now turn,* her mind instructed her wrist.

As another man began to climb out, the first man neared her. She slowly squatted down. "Don't come near me." She turned, climbed out of her window, and stood on the small ledge as one of the men approached the window.

"You're going to get hurt. Please come back in. We wouldn't want you to fall. No one is going to hurt you."

Says every killer.

There were now four men in the room and two of them were pointing pistols at her.

They're going to shoot me?

One of the men knelt to climb out after her. Farmer clicked her heels together, and her shoes lit up. She looked down and stepped off the ledge, catching her breath. She bent her knees and dropped a few feet before gliding through the air toward the SkyTran.

I'm coming, Halland. Please don't fall.

CHAPTER 62

"Look," Aiden yelled as they ran.

Halland teetered on the rail with men carefully stepping toward him. One of them reached him and extended a hand. "Come on, kid. We just want to get you down from here."

"You're lying," said Halland.

Just as the other men got close enough to reach for him, Halland looked down and lost his footing. The closest man grabbed him and pulled him back onto the rail.

"See that? We almost lost you there, son."

"I'm not your son," Halland yelled as he tried punching him. Halland was smarter than most adults, and his voice was deep for his age, but he only had the body of a twelve-year-old, and his punches weren't enough to do any damage.

The man dragged him toward the others. "Stop struggling. You're going to make us both fall, and I can't have that."

Halland reached up and accidentally jabbed the man in the eye, causing him to loosen his grip, and then purposely jabbed him in the other eye.

The man yelled out, releasing him. Halland fell back, his arms flailing as he teetered and grabbed onto the man's belt to keep from falling. Halland's weight pulled the man off balance, and they fell over the side of the rail.

The man grabbed hold of the rail. Halland hung below him, still holding his belt, but began to slip as it broke away from the man. He screamed as he fell.

"Gotcha!" Farmer exclaimed as she grabbed Halland in midair, her arms wrapped tightly around his waist. "Hold on."

"Hurry," Halland yelled.

He still held the object from the man's belt and lifted it up for her to see. "Throw it!" yelled Farmer. The men on the SkyTran rail now held guns aimed at them.

Halland pushed the button on top of the explosive and threw it as hard as he could.

Farmer pressed her feet forward to pick up speed and headed toward the other Sleepers.

The bomb went off, and the blast propelled them forward.

It was as if the explosion ripped the sky apart. Debris showered all around them as the SkyTran crashed to the ground. The Sleepers were thrown off their feet.

Aiden crawled over to where Farmer and Halland landed. Farmer lay on her side. "Farmer," he called. She lifted her head. Aiden rolled her toward him and held her as she tried to sit up.

"I can't stand, Aiden. I can't move my leg at all." Blood soaked through her pant leg, the material torn, revealing a large gash.

Halland gasped as he scrambled over to Farmer, seeing how badly she was injured. His face and hands were scraped up, but otherwise, he was okay. Farmer had taken the brunt of the fall. "Farmer, I'm sorry."

"It's not your fault," she replied with a moan.

Halland wiped his brow. "What you did was crazy amazing. Thank you."

The Sleepers gathered together helping each other to stand. The area took on a grey hue as if it were dusk.

"Why is it so dark in the middle of the day?" asked Fitz.

"We need to go," said Aiden. "We'll have to carry her."

"There's so much smoke," Danai said as she applied pressure to Farmer's leg, tying her sock around it.

"Grab any sharp object that may be useable as a weapon. They're not done with us," said Bale.

"Which way?" asked Lax. He helped Aiden bring Farmer to a standing position and braced her on his shoulder to take the weight off her leg.

As the smoke cleared, they looked around and gasped. Halland's voice shook. "Where the heck are we?"

The blast had caused the device the facility used to disguise its identity to malfunction. There were fluctuations as the system attempted to get back online and transform to the look of the Institute campus.

The whole place was surrounded by an energy field that resembled the dimpled pattern of a golf ball. "We were never outside at all. We were inside this thing the whole time."

Everyone turned, taking in the full facility. There was nowhere to run. Everything had disappeared—manicured lawns, buildings, and outdoor facilities. It had all been an illusion. Left in its place was a mile-long building that surrounded them on every side. Their dorm suites were nothing more than cages, the window side open to whatever technician was studying them for the day.

Aiden remembered that day he saw the sun in the wrong place and realized it was never really the sun. That's why the elevators never felt like they were lowering or rising. They weren't.

Security surrounded them along with the student sims.

"What are we going to do?" Danai yelled.

"Aiden?" said Fitz. His eyes pleaded with him.

Aiden's mind raced. What *could* they do? After all they had been through, they hadn't come up with anything that could save them. They had abilities that were of no use at all when they were awake. *They looked to me as a leader, and I've failed them.*

"Make the circle," instructed Lax.

"We only did that in the visionscope."

"Do it," yelled Quest. "We have to try."

Farmer took Aiden's hand on the right, followed by Lax. Danai took his hand on the left. They made a circle with Farmer still leaning on Lax.

"Nothing's happening."

"Close your eyes, Aiden. Focus. It's on you."

Aiden closed his eyes as the men with guns moved toward them. He blocked everything out and focused on the Sleepers.

The other Sleepers looked down at their hands as they began to feel a tingling sensation. They closed their eyes. The same force they'd experienced in the vision-scope shot out of them, throwing them back onto the ground, knocking down those that were closing in on them and short-circuiting the sims.

"We did it," yelled Halland. "We did it while awake!"

"Yeah, but does anyone else feel drained now?" asked Tristan.

"We have to try to get out of here," yelled Fitz, helping Danai up.

Bale stopped moving. "Something's happening."

The portion of ground they stood upon began to shake. "What now?" yelled Quest as they closed in toward each other.

"We need to get out of here right now," Bale yelled to Aiden. Aiden agreed, but before they could move, the ground began to lower, rocking them off their feet. Lax fell to one side and Aiden to the other, catching Farmer.

"Go, get out of here," he yelled at the others.

They were too late. Tristan tried to grab onto the edge of the ground and pull himself up, but it gave way.

The ground lowered into a chamber filled with gas. The mist wafted over them. Lax tried to hold his breath but fell to his knees, choking after breathing in too much of the mist.

Aiden fell back, feeling the cold, hard ground beneath him, and the weight of Farmer's body slumped over him.

All around him, the Sleepers' bodies went limp, surrendering to the sedative.

As Aiden's eyes closed, he noticed a metallic taste in his mouth, and as he inhaled, his nostrils burned. He fought to open his eyes. Squinting, he could just barely make out the blurry image of an opening. Men in white hazmat suits with gas masks that covered their entire heads wheeled in exam tables. He watched two of them pick up Halland, place him on a table, and wheel him out. Within seconds, nothing but darkness and silence surrounded him.

CHAPTER 63

MRS. QUINN

"How long have we been walking?" asked Coulter.

"I don't know, but the GPS tracker still shows we are heading in the right direction," Mrs. Quinn replied.

They came to an abrupt stop. Coulter tilted his head. "That's one huge fan. What do you say, about fifteen feet?"

"Yeah, but that's all there is. How is the tracker telling us to go straight ahead?"

Coulter looked up. "Through there."

"Are you kidding me?"

"I can hoist you up."

"You know what? I'm not even going to argue. I'm tired, and we don't have any other choice."

Coulter stepped next to the wall, leaned forward, and weaved his fingers together to hoist her up. "Okay, step on, and then head for my shoulders."

"Are you sure you can hold me?"

"I'm stronger than I look."

"You'd better be." Mrs. Quinn stepped into his hands and bounced a couple of times before pushing up off his hands.

Coulter grunted as he pushed higher. "Get on my shoulders!"

Mrs. Quinn began to wobble, her pelvis smashed against Coulter's face. *This is so freaking awkward.*

"Hurry, climb!"

"Okay, I'm climbing." She put one knee on his shoulder and then the other. "Don't let me fall, Coulter!"

Her buttocks were over his head. "Please don't fart. You have to stand," he groaned.

"I'm trying to." Her voice was high-pitched and breathy. She wobbled as she pressed against the wall and slowly rose to stand. "Okay, okay. Made it."

"Pull yourself up!"

Mrs. Quinn inhaled, reached into the vent hole, and grunted like she was lifting a heavy weight as she pulled herself up. Coulter pushed her by the feet, and she pulled until she lay on her stomach catching her breath, her feet hanging out of the hole.

"Hello up there," Coulter sang.

"Okay, I'm ready," she strained out. "How are we going to do this?"

Coulter looked around the tunnel. "I don't know."

"It was your idea."

"I know. I'm just joking. Get ready to catch me."

"Catch you?"

Before she could say anything else, Coulter ran to the other side of the tunnel, hopped up and down a few times, and took off at a full sprint toward the wall. He jumped up, slamming the side of his face into the wall under the vent hole.

"Ow!" Coulter exclaimed as he dropped down.

"What did you do that for?"

"I saw it in a movie. I thought I could do it."

"Are you okay?"

"No," he said with a muffled voice as he held his face. "Let me try it again."

"No, Aiden—I mean, Coulter. Sheesh, you and Aiden act just alike."

Coulter took off running again, and this time when he jumped, Mrs. Quinn held her crossbody bag out of the hole and Coulter grabbed it.

"Use your feet to climb," she yelled as she pulled on the bag, pressing her back against the wall and her feet against the opposite wall. "Hurry, one of the straps is breaking."

Coulter climbed into the opening and collapsed over Mrs. Quinn's lap, his lower half still hanging out of the hole.

"Give me a minute. I can't feel my arms."

Mrs. Quinn crawled through the small space. "There's light ahead," she said as she peered out of the tunnel and to the left. To the right was a brick wall. Following the dim light, she emerged from the tunnel and carefully stood, her knees aching from crawling for so long.

"We were right. This is a ventilation shaft." She pointed. "There's another tunnel on that side. And if I'm not mistaken," she shone the flashlight behind the other tunnel, "there should be a door just about here." She walked up to the dark area, shining her light on the door handle, then turned the knob and peered inside. "Yep, emergency access stairs."

Coulter grimaced.

Mrs. Quinn shone the light on his face.

"How is it?" he asked.

"Scratches, bruise, you'll live." She smiled. "The pain is a good thing. It will keep you alert. You want Mama to kiss it to make it better?"

"Heck no." He pushed a button on his wristband, checking the tracker. "We're not far from Aiden's CPU wallet."

"We're not going to the wallet."

"Why not?"

"Aiden doesn't keep it on him. It's probably in his room, and he wouldn't be there right now." She opened the holomap again. "The facility is below ground, so we shouldn't have many steps to climb."

"What's at the top?"

"There must be tons of ventilation equipment above us. I would guess some type of work center or mechanical room is up there for dealing with air and everything." She turned to face Coulter. "This is it. Are you ready?"

"No, but this is as ready as I'm going to get. When we find him, how are we going to get out?"

"I'm sure we'll figure out something."

Coulter and Mrs. Quinn climbed four stories up the metal stairs before arriving at the steel door at the top. Mrs. Quinn slowly turned the knob. "It's not locked," she whispered. She opened the door. "A mechanical room, just as I'd thought."

"Why is no one in here?"

"I don't know." Mrs. Quinn held Jaxxon's pistol at her side and looked around. "Coulter, quick. Can we use any of this equipment to pinpoint where he is?"

Coulter stepped in front of the CPU unit and looked it over. His mouth twisted to the side as he chewed on the inside of his cheek. "Okay," he said as his fingers went to work on the virtual keyboard. Images around the facility appeared in front of them.

Mrs. Quinn's eyes jumped around the images. "Good going. You're in."

"There are soldiers everywhere."

Mrs. Quinn turned away from him, looking around the room. She searched the lockers at the back wall and took two jackets from one of them. She handed one to Coulter. "Here, put this on. Wait," she exclaimed. "What's that? Where is that?" She pointed at the screen.

Men glided tables with bodies on them into a room.

Coulter's eyes widened. "Do you think—"

"Get us there, Coulter."

Mrs. Quinn turned and froze in place as if she would fall through ice if she moved. She closed her eyes. "Something's wrong."

"You think so? I mean, look at everything we've been—" Coulter turned to her and stood. "What is it?"

"I think—Do you smell—Is that seawater? It's Aiden. We need to hurry."

Moby Dick.

CHAPTER 64

MS. GENOVA

Ms. Genova sat at her office desk, wishing she were anywhere but there. Due to the alarm, every teacher was made to stay within their class or office. There was a lot of commotion on campus, but she couldn't get anyone to tell her what was going on.

She pushed a button on her desk.

A robotic voice came through the speakers on her wall. "Yes, Ms. Genova."

"My door is locked," she stated as she stood and paced back and forth in front of her desk. She shook her hands in front of her. "I don't like feeling confined like this."

"It's for your own safety, professor. The door will unlock as soon as we remove the threat from the campus."

Ms. Genova frowned. *What kind of threat could it be? Did a student have a weapon on campus?* She looked around the small office. As much work as she did for the Institute, one would think she would be rewarded with an office with a window. She felt trapped. With the system down, she couldn't even surf through her favorite websites while she waited.

Suddenly, everything that wasn't bolted down in the room slid toward the back wall. She yelled out as she fell back onto the floor, pinned by her desk. It was as if the building lifted at an angle, and then slammed down.

Ms. Genova pushed the furniture away from her and ran to the office door. *I've got to get out of here.* Yanking and banging on the door did nothing to free her. "Let me out of here!"

She tried to look down the corridor through the small window. She could just make out a figure approaching.

Professor Houser stopped, seeing her, and motioned for her to back up. He took a blade from his pocket and began working on the lock. "Stand back," he yelled. He took a few steps back and kicked hard at the door, busting it open.

Ms. Genova didn't know whether to be thankful or afraid. "Why do you have that?"

"It's just a Swiss knife I grabbed from my desk. Look, the blade isn't even sharp," he said, running it over the palm of his hand.

"What's going on out there? Why was I locked in?"

Professor Houser stepped toward her, and she stepped back.

"You have no reason to be afraid of me. I came to get you out of here. I don't know what they'll do to you if I leave you."

"They? Who? What are you talking about?" She looked into his eyes. "You're a part of it, aren't you—whatever's going on here?"

"No, I am not. But we've got to get out of here and find those kids. Do you know where they are?"

"What do you mean? Has something happened to my students?"

"There's no time to explain. Where?"

Ms. Genova fell toward the wall as the building began to shake. "The labs. If they've been taken, I believe they've been taken somewhere for tests."

She watched his eyes widen.

"I think I know where," he stated as he turned to leave the room.

"Wait, I'm going with you," she announced as she followed behind him. "Did we just have an earthquake or a tornado?" They turned down the passage and turned again to get to the main hall.

"No. We need to get down to the lower levels."

"What do you mean, no? Buildings don't move by themselves, and what lower levels? There's only one floor below the main one," Ms. Genova stated.

"That's what they want you to think." Professor Houser turned toward the stairs and stopped. "What's that sound?"

Ms. Genova kept running forward down the hall.

"Where are you going?"

"The service elevator," she yelled over her shoulder.

"You'll never make it—" His eyes widened. "This isn't possible," he said as he looked behind Ms. Genova.

"What?" was all he heard from her as she was hit by a wave of ice-cold seawater. It rushed down the hall and swept Ms. Genova toward the back wall.

Professor Houser grabbed her as the wave pulled them underwater toward the stairs. He fought against the churning water and held to the stair railing as it rushed down the stairs around them.

Ms. Genova, shivering and coughing from choking, held to the railing as Professor Houser pushed them forward out of the flow to the level below.

They sloshed through the dimly-lit corridor. "What the heck is going on?" Ms. Genova asked.

"Something they didn't count on."

"Who didn't count on?"

"Come on, we have to get to the elevator."

Ms. Genova turned. "Do you hear that?" she whispered.

Professor Houser stopped moving. A low moan came from behind them. "Walk carefully," he whispered. "Try not to splash. If I yell go, run as fast as you can to the elevator and don't look back."

Ms. Genova nodded while brushing wet strands of hair out of her face. She looked up. The ceiling sounded as if it were shifting from the weight of the water. It creaked and popped as water began to leak through crevices. Little waves spread around them as they moved through the knee-high flood.

Professor Houser tapped on her back. She stopped walking and turned to look at him. He held a finger up to his mouth and stretched his other hand toward her. She understood and didn't make a sound, nor move.

They heard humanlike screeching. Suddenly, a zombie-like creature was standing there, looking at them.

"Go," Houser yelled.

Ms. Genova ran as fast as she could through the water, falling in front of the elevator door. It sounded as if there were hundreds of the monsters chasing them. Houser banged hard on the button and picked her up. The doors opened, and he threw her into the elevator, slamming her into the back wall.

"Close, close, close," Ms. Genova chanted and cried at the same time.

Professor Houser banged on the button, trying to hurry the door. It closed just as the creatures reached the door.

"I don't understand what's going on," she cried. We're flooding like we're on the Titanic, and what were those things? Zombies?"

Professor Houser didn't respond. He placed his hand near the door and a red light scanned across his wrist. The elevator began to move.

"What was that scan? Wh-where is this going?" asked Ms. Genova as she shivered.

A red light ticked down toward the floor.

"Are those floors? What's on these other floors?"

Professor Houser didn't answer. The elevator door opened, and armed men stood before them. The closest one spoke to Professor Houser. "What's happening up there, Sir?"

"Get as many men as you can to the main level. Save all that you can," Houser replied.

Ms. Genova looked at the soldier. "Who are you? What's going on here?"

"You'll learn everything soon enough." He beckoned to the other soldiers, and they crammed into the elevator and closed the door.

A siren blared as people ran by, totally ignoring the two sopping wet people they passed. "What are they doing?" Ms. Genova asked.

"Evacuating."

A young girl Ms. Genova recognized ran up to them. "Houser. I've been looking for you—"

"Get to the rendezvous point."

She nodded and ran in the opposite direction.

They went door to door, Houser scanning his wrist with the clearance to get them into lab after lab, looking for the Sleepers. To their surprise, inside the next lab they entered, they found Mrs. Quinn already there with a boy helping her wake the students. Two technicians lie on the ground, either dead or unconscious.

"Help me wake them," Mrs. Quinn yelled, seeing Ms. Genova.

They rushed around the room, shaking the students. Each student lay with electrodes attached to their heads, with a green energy arc closed over them.

Ms. Genova looked up, hearing footsteps rush in. "Dr. Laribe!"

He looked around the room, holding onto his bleeding arm. "What can I do?"

"Wake them," Mrs. Quinn yelled.

"What happened to you?" asked Ms. Genova.

"Werewolves."

CHAPTER 65

Waking the Sleepers was a hard task. They'd quickly gone into a deep REM state after inhaling the serum mist.

Dr. Laribe yelled into Danai's face and shook her. He lifted her torso, shook her, and laid her down again. "Wake up!"

Danai grimaced and raised her hand to her face.

Dr. Laribe looked over at Professor Houser rousing Fitz, and then around the room, making sure everyone was okay. He stood with his back to Aiden's table. "Looks like they're all awake."

Some of the Sleepers were beginning to sit up. Ms. Genova assisted them, removing the electrodes from their heads.

"Can someone please explain to me what's going on?" asked Dr. Laribe.

"Maybe you would like to explain how someone who doesn't know what's going on has security clearance to get down to a level of the facility that doesn't exist," demanded Professor Houser.

Mrs. Quinn and Ms. Genova both looked at him.

Aiden mumbled something. Mrs. Quinn walked around Dr. Laribe, pushing him out of the way. Aiden's eyes were slightly open, and he mumbled slurred sounds.

"What's wrong, baby?" She lifted his head. "What is it?" she asked in Spanish.

Everyone fell off their feet as the room shook and began to shift. Mrs. Quinn pulled herself back up to Aiden's side.

"Aiden!" He didn't move nor look at her. "Aiden? Oh my God! He was never awake," she yelled. A corner of a building shot out of the floor and up through the ceiling at the front of the lab. She threw her body over Aiden to shield him as a barrage of projectiles flew in every direction.

Professor Houser dove at Mrs. Quinn and Aiden, knocking over the table with them on it, so they could duck behind it. Everyone scrambled, taking cover under or behind the exam tables.

"What did you do to him?" Mrs. Quinn yelled at Dr. Laribe.

Dr. Laribe looked confused. "I didn't do this."

Mrs. Quinn held Aiden to her chest. "Bring him out!"

Coulter's eyes widened as he watched the wall that jutted from the lab. The building began to change and twist around. "He's going to tear the Institute apart. Wake him up!" yelled Coulter.

Mrs. Quinn didn't know what to do. "He's too far under," she yelled as the ceiling began to cave in. She watched his eyes quickly dart back and forth under his lids.

With a shaky voice, Mrs. Quinn began to sing a song she used to sing to Aiden when he was a small boy.

"You can come home," she sang.

The singing seemed to reach Aiden somewhere in the deepest recesses of his mind. The shifting of the building slowed, but it wasn't enough to bring him out.

Farmer looked down at her bracelets, and then over at Aiden. She remembered his words, "Tell me about your bracelets." *I'll show you*, she thought as she crawled over to him and his mother with her wounded leg stretched out behind her. Mrs. Quinn watched her as she removed several of the glowing beads of bracelets from her wrist and placed them on Aiden's arm.

Mrs. Quinn fought back tears. It was a gesture people often did when someone was dying, to give them something of value to them. Tears fell as reality sunk in that they were really going to die. Then she watched the girl.

Farmer pulled one of the bracelets away from Aiden's skin. As it contracted toward his arm, it reacted with the other beads, causing a shock. Aiden jumped but didn't wake.

"Help me," said Farmer. Mrs. Quinn pulled two of the strands in opposite directions, and Farmer pulled the other two. "Now," said Farmer. They both let go of the bracelets and watched a flow of current run up Aiden's arm.

Aiden's eyes flew open.

Mrs. Quinn placed her hand on Farmer's arm and smiled at her. "It worked."

Danai screamed.

Dr. Laribe held a pistol pointed at Mrs. Quinn. "I have to have those readings."

Professor Houser lunged at him. They fought, falling over a table. Lax ran forward and tried pulling on Dr. Laribe's fingers, grimacing as he tugged. He then bit into Dr. Laribe's hand and grabbed the pistol as Quest and Bale ran over to help him.

Tristan picked up an instrument and ran forward. "Houser, move!" He slammed it down on Dr. Laribe's legs. Dr. Laribe cried out as his head fell back into the water that flowed into the room from the ceiling. He began to dissolve before their eyes. His face glowed and sizzled as electric currents shot across his head. Another image focused in and out on his face until what had been a mask totally short-circuited.

Mrs. Quinn stood and looked at him. "General Sherin? The Secretary of Defense? You're behind this? The government is behind this?"

He smirked, and Professor Houser punched him in the face, knocking him out. They all stared down at him as Aiden fully roused.

"Move. We've got to go," said Professor Houser. He took the sidearm from Lax and searched the general's pockets. He found what he was looking for. "We've got one magazine of bullets. I have a way out, but we've got to go now."

"How?" asked Mrs. Quinn.

"I work for someone who has known about you all along and sent me to look out for you," Houser replied.

"Who?"

"Look, General Sherin may have come here alone, looking like some kind of knight in shining armor as part of Dr. Laribe's charade, but I guarantee you his soldiers are not far off. Follow me."

Professor Houser led them to a passage to the underground railway Mrs. Quinn and Coulter had climbed.

They ducked, hearing shots fired from behind them.

"Which way do we go?" asked Fitz

"This way. Come on," yelled Bale.

Mrs. Quinn looked at him, surprised. "How do you know?"

"I just feel it."

"Yes, go through there," Professor Houser yelled as he pushed them forward and fired back at the men.

"Houser!" Ms. Genova screamed.

He turned to see Halland falling back, his back arched and his chest pushing forward, arms stretched back behind him.

"Take them through that opening," Houser yelled as he scrambled over to Halland, who was moaning, his eyes open and searching the ceiling. "Go. Now!"

"Where does it lead?" Ms. Genova asked.

"Away from this facility."

Ms. Genova ran to catch up with the rest of the Sleepers as they hurried through the dark passage.

Aiden looked around. "Where's Halland?"

"Houser's helping him," Ms. Genova responded, thinking against offering any more information than that.

"What? You left him?"

"Aiden!" yelled Mrs. Quinn as she pulled at him.

He broke free of her grasp and stumbled away from her.

"Aiden," she yelled again. Coulter ran after him, followed by Farmer, limping, as she pulled away from Tristan.

"Farmer, no," said Tristan.

"Let me go."

Mrs. Quinn turned to Ms. Genova. "Keep going. We'll get them."

CHAPTER 66

Ms. Genova and the other Sleepers followed Houser's direction and ran through the tunnel. The area was lit by small bulbs every few feet, situated near the ceiling to the right.

Lax held a hand up, and everyone slowed. "There's an opening ahead, quiet."

They walked carefully and slowly to the opening and looked out at a girl who stood with a semi-automatic weapon drawn at them. She stood on a platform in front of a rail line.

Lax stepped forward. "Brooks?"

She didn't lower the weapon. "Where is Aiden and everyone else?"

"They're back there. They told us to keep going." Lax kept walking toward her.

"Don't move," she yelled.

Lax stopped.

The other Sleepers stood back near the tunnel, watching in shock.

"Are you with them, Brooks? Are you really going to shoot me?"

Gunfire echoed through the tunnel.

"Everyone over there," she yelled, moving the weapon in the direction they needed to go.

Lax didn't take his eyes off her. "It was all just a game, huh? Aiden saw right through you from the start. Did you get what you wanted? How old are you, anyway?"

Brooks slowly turned, putting her back toward the tunnel exit. Lax turned as she turned. Now that the Sleepers and Ms. Genova had stepped off to the side, she began to back toward the opening.

A tear dropped from her eye. "Wait here, a rescue team is coming for you."

She turned into the tunnel, but Lax yelled out to her. "Where are you going?"

Brooks sighed and shook her head as if she were trying to stop herself from doing something. "I'm eighteen, and I'm going to save your friends." She turned and ran through the tunnel.

Lax watched her until she disappeared into the darkness.

"I loved you, Lax," she yelled behind her.

Lax took off running after her.

"Lax, no! Don't!" yelled Tristan.

Quest and Oui yelled out for him to stop.

"Stay there," Lax yelled back.

CHAPTER 67

"**Y**ou guys shouldn't be here!" Houser yelled.

"You can reprimand us later," Aiden responded while dropping down next to Halland.

Halland's eyes opened slightly, and he breathed heavily.

"We're going to get you out of here. We're a team, remember?"

Halland tried to nod, but his head barely moved.

Coulter approached and ducked down. "Can we carry him?"

"We have to try."

"I'll cover you," said Houser. "But move quickly. I'm almost out of ammo."

A moan came from Halland as Aiden and Coulter lifted him to sit upright. They put his arms over each of their shoulders just as Farmer approached them.

"What are you doing?" asked Aiden.

"I was worried about—"

Shots rang out. Houser ducked. Bullets shot across from three different angles around the mouth of the tunnel.

They had nothing to hide behind. They could only lower themselves to the ground or against the wall.

Some of the soldiers moved in closer, while others fired.

Farmer screamed.

Aiden's eyes widened as he watched her fall. "No!"

Halland slid out of his arms as they dove to the side. Houser dashed toward them while firing behind him.

She's asleep. She's just asleep, Aiden thought as he frantically crawled to Farmer. His eyes were so blurry with tears, he couldn't see. He shook as he removed the bracelets from his arm, placed them on hers and snapped them on her skin. Nothing happened. She didn't move. "Farmer!" he screamed as he felt two hands grab him under his armpits. His mother pulled at him. He screamed hysterically as he looked down at Farmer.

Coulter was now pushing him back as he fought, and Houser grabbed him. "Run," he yelled. "I'm out of ammo."

Aiden's eyes widened as he recognized Brooks running from behind them with a semi-automatic weapon, shooting at the soldiers.

"Go," yelled Brooks as Lax appeared behind them. Lax stopped, seeing Halland and Farmer on the ground.

"Brooks, come on," yelled Lax. "I won't leave you."

Soldiers charged toward them. Brooks jumped in front of Lax, falling back toward him. She continued shooting as Lax caught her. Soldiers fell to the ground. Her rifle dropped from her hands. She looked up at Lax.

"Go," was all he heard before noticing her bullet wounds.

He carefully laid her down and backed away.

Brooks grunted and turned on her side, her fingers reaching out, trying to get to her rifle. Soldiers were moving in closer.

Suddenly, the rifle slammed into her hands as if she had summoned it there. She looked back and saw Lax's feet and then up at his hand still outstretched toward the rifle.

"Go!" she yelled and began firing as Lax ran as fast as he could, tears streaming down his face.

CHAPTER 68

Mrs. Quinn, Coulter, and Professor Houser emerged from the tunnel, dragging Aiden. Lax followed close behind. A rush of air shot from the left of them as a bullet train pulled forward and stopped directly in front of the platform. Soldiers, wearing berets and grey camouflage uniforms, stormed out of the train.

Houser turned, hearing feet bounding through the tunnel. "Get in," he yelled as the soldiers ushered them into a car, and then lined up on the platform, shooting at those in pursuit of them. "Go!" one of them yelled.

The train engine revved as if it were building up a powerful force and shot off like a rocket, throwing them backward off their feet. There they stayed, due to the speed of the train, until it slowed.

Aiden grabbed hold of the side of a seat and slowly lifted himself from the ground. "Here, Mom," he said, taking her hand and pulling her to her feet.

Everyone found a seat except for the soldiers, whose job, it seemed, was to stand guard at the rear, front, and specific areas throughout the car.

The train slowed almost to a stop. They felt a bump and a shift in the front end. *It's disconnecting from the other cars,* thought Aiden.

Through the glass panels at the front, he saw the cars ahead of them switch to another track as they began moving up.

Aiden looked over at Fitz, holding tight to the handrail next to him. The train felt like a rollercoaster rising to its highest peak.

"I don't think I like where this is going," yelled Coulter. But the train quickly leveled off and continued down another track.

"Since when do trains climb mountains?" Quest stated. He wasn't really asking a question.

Houser stood and looked out a window. He saw Fitz staring at him and patted him on the shoulder. "You made it. You kids are finally safe."

"Is it true?" whispered Tristan to Bale. "Are we safe? Do you sense it?"

Bale nodded hesitantly.

The Sleepers watched him but didn't say a word. They didn't immediately have the good feeling they should have had after being rescued from their captors. There were no celebratory bumping of fists or cheers. They were mostly in shock about everything they had seen and endured. The loss of people they cared about, Dr. Laribe's true identity, and that Houser, and then Brooks, came to their rescue.

Lax and Aiden held similar painful expressions, overloaded with emotion and turmoil. Motionless, their eyes staring ahead at the front of the train, they relived most of the past hour.

CHAPTER 69

Where are they taking us? Aiden wondered. The Sleepers looked like they were returning from the front lines of a war, and some needed medical attention.

In the seat ahead of him, Aiden noticed Bale's head drop to the side. He leaned forward, trying to see his face.

It caught Houser's attention. "Did he pass out? Is he asleep?" he asked as he approached the boy. He knelt next to him. "Bale!"

Bale didn't respond. Now all the Sleepers were sitting up and looking at Bale. Houser lifted his head and patted him gently on the jaw. "Bale."

"He's asleep," said Aiden. "You have to wake him up."

"He just fell asleep. How much harm could it do?" Houser asked.

"Believe me, you don't want to find out," said Mrs. Quinn.

As she spoke, gunfire erupted from outside the train. Everyone ducked and laid on the floor.

"It's him. Wake him up!" yelled Danai.

Houser aggressively shook Bale just as an explosive hit the back of the train. Aiden grimaced at the sound of metal twisting as it tore the back of the train clear off. Soldiers yelled out as the blast wounded and propelled some forward and sucked others out.

Aiden felt himself being pulled back and tried to reach out and grab the base of a seat. Mrs. Quinn, also holding onto the base, tried to grab for Aiden. As he slid back, Lax's hand clasped over his wrist. Lax gritted his teeth. He pulled Aiden just as the shockwave reversed, tossing them both into the opposite wall, waking Bale.

"What the heck goes on in you kids' minds?" groaned Houser as he stood, making sure everyone was okay.

CHAPTER 70

The bullet train, or what was left of it, went on for miles. For some reason, Aiden thought that wherever they were going would be a much quicker trip. But then, why would they make it that easy on anyone who pursued them? And who was this person that had been secretly looking out for them? Who else could possibly know about them?

His heart skipped a beat. *What if it's my dad?* It was possible. He hadn't seen his father for years, but what if the man had still been looking out for him?

He licked the inside of his mouth, tasting salt. *I'm bleeding. I hope I don't lose a tooth.*

The ride was jerky due to what was left of the car, but they were sailing along faster than any normal train. Actually, normal and train couldn't be used here. *This thing climbed. But to where?* Aiden laid his head on the headrest. This was not how he thought the day would end.

He pictured the Sleepers climbing over the main gate and running up the stairs to the Teslaloop station, anxiously awaiting the next capsule, riding the travelator to his home, calling all the Sleepers later that night—no, maybe one in particular—and then sleeping in his own sleep chamber. Instead, they sat riddled with shrapnel and dirt, covered with scrapes and cuts, mourning.

His mother's fingers tightened through his, and he glanced at her. She placed her other hand over his bicep, intuitively knowing her embrace would add the warmth that seemed to be seeping away from his body.

"Danai," he said. *What's wrong with my voice? My mouth must be swelling.* "Mom, get her. She's falling asleep." Mrs. Quinnn reached out and shook her. Danai raised her hand to show that she was awake.

"Look," Fitz exclaimed.

They all leaned forward and stared ahead. The area they approached was bright and filled with light. Daylight. Aiden would have smiled if he could. But his heart wouldn't let him. The other Sleepers were pleased to see the light that engulfed the area. It was as if sunlight was the answer to the pain and darkest places that existed within them. It went hand in hand with their freedom.

There was no guarantee they were truly safe, nor that they wouldn't be hunted. But at that moment, they stared ahead at a light that made them feel redeemed. A light that said, *this is your reward for what you've been through. I will shine upon you, and it will strengthen and renew you.*

Aiden looked to the rear, through the open area that looked as if the back had been bitten off by a giant shark. *Okay, that's a thought I don't need. Get that visual out of your mind.*

The train lurched ahead, leaving the nightmare in the dark passage behind him. *Here's a better visual*, he thought as he turned forward. *Inhabitants of Middle Sun, your human king has returned.*

BUT THERE'S MORE...

Please Leave A Review

Your review means the world to me. I greatly appreciate any kind words. Even one or two sentences go a long way. Thank you in advance.

Check Out the Next Book

The Eleven

They shouldn't have brought us together.
We are more powerful than they could ever have imagined.

ABOUT THE AUTHOR

Auri Blest is the pen name of best-selling middle grade fiction author L. B. Anne. She resides in Seminole, Florida with her husband and enjoys inspiring young adults through fantasy, science fiction, and suspense. Auri engages both heart and mind with stories that draw from her own life experiences, a vivid imagination, and a love for all things science, technology, and adventure related.

Stay in touch at lbanne.com/auriblestbooks

Facebook: facebook.com/auriblestauthor

Made in the USA
Las Vegas, NV
03 December 2024

13230209R00142